For Chris

Wallace E. Clendann

Enjoy!
With love,
Pat Clendenen

Abiding Love

One Woman's Journey through Prohibition, the Depression, and World War II

Wallace E. Clendenen

iUniverse, Inc.
New York   Bloomington

Abiding Love

One Woman's Journey through Prohibition, the Depression, and World War II

This is a work of fiction. All of the characters, names, incidents, organizations, and dialogue in this novel are either the products of the author's imagination or are used fictitiously.

iUniverse books may be ordered through booksellers or by contacting:

iUniverse
1663 Liberty Drive
Bloomington, IN 47403
www.iuniverse.com
1-800-Authors (1-800-288-4677)

Because of the dynamic nature of the Internet, any Web addresses or links contained in this book may have changed since publication and may no longer be valid. The views expressed in this work are solely those of the author and do not necessarily reflect the views of the publisher, and the publisher hereby disclaims any responsibility for them.

ISBN: 978-0-595-47941-2 (pbk)
ISBN:978-0-595-49524-5 (cloth)
ISBN: 978-1-4401-0837-2 (ebk)

Printed in the United States of America

iUniverse Rev. 11/12/2008

And now faith, hope, and love abide, these three;

and the greatest of these is love.

- I Corinthians 13:13

Acknowledgments

To my wife, Ede, who spent hours typing, correcting my spelling and punctuations, and the even more difficult task of trying to read my writing.

To my son-in-law, Sven-Erik Hansson, for his photography work.

A special thanks to my daughter, Patricia Clendenen, who did all the detail work in preparing the manuscript for publication. Without her help, this book would never have been published.

Chapter I

Ellen stood at the open grave and marveled at how much remained the same from when she was here almost twenty years ago, only fifteen then and just beginning to fill out. She remembered how her breasts strained at the cotton print dress and all the trouble she had pulling it over her hips.

It was the lean years of the Depression. Her mother knew the dress was too small, but simply didn't have enough money to buy her a new one.

Looking about her, Ellen saw the same brown grass and swirling dust she had endured twenty years earlier. The dust had irritated her tear-filled eyes, and the wind had wound her long blonde hair around her face.

Her heart was breaking and the future frightening and lonely at best. They were there to bury her father and she knew that, without him, her life would never be the same.

Now, twenty years later, on the advice of Brad, a close friend and practicing psychiatrist, Ellen returned to this place, a new widow of thirty-five. She had come to bury her husband of only five years. Their life together had been good in spite of the age difference. He had been thirty years her senior and had died two days after celebrating his sixty-fifth year.

A lot had happened to Ellen in twenty years. The man she was here to bury was her third husband. The only one of her husbands still living was the first, whom she had married when she was nineteen. Brad had told her that, if she ever expected to have a real life she must first come back to this place and bury her husband and also her past.

He had been right. Her life had begun when her father was buried on this spot. She had been carrying too much excess baggage the last twenty years and needed to bring it back here and bury it. However, knowing he was right did not make it any easier to face the painful episodes from her past.

The changes about Ellen were so insignificant it made it hard for her to separate the things from the past from what was happening at present. The cars still raced along the road just outside the cemetery fence; there were just more of them now and the increased noise was more disturbing.

The preacher droned on and on, just as he had twenty years earlier. Ellen could remember thinking, "If Dad were not already dead, this guy would bore him to death."

She had often wondered if preachers thought they were paid by the word. There was one difference between her father's experience and that of H.T. He had been a Methodist and Methodists disliked long sermons, but H.T. had been of the Church of God and they enjoyed sermons long and loud. Ellen could remember spending too many Sundays listening to long-winded sermons, when the time could have been better spent in bed.

What had not changed from the first time she was here was the attention of the men. At her father's funeral, as they carried the casket to place it over the open grave, the pallbearer in front caught sight of that tight cotton dress glued to her hips, raised his eyes, and zeroed in on her nipples trying to punch holes in the bodice. He suddenly caught his toe in the artificial turf and almost pitched headfirst into the open grave. The only thing that saved him was the man behind him who grabbed his coattail.

Today, standing beside the grave, that fifteen-year-old beauty had not faded, but had simply matured. Ellen was still a honey blonde, but now her hair was fashioned by the best experts money could obtain. The cotton print dress was replaced by a black silk dress, a one-of-a-kind creation just for her.

Ellen was a very beautiful woman. That would have been evident even in the print dress she wore at age fifteen, or in nothing at all. Yet, it still came as a surprise to her when one of the men, concentrating on her and not where he was going, caught his toe and nearly pitched headfirst into the open grave. As before, an accident was averted when the man behind him grabbed his coattail.

Her friend Dot had once said to her, "Ellen, get used to it. Any man who is a real man will never be able to resist undressing you with his eyes."

She had often wondered if her life might have been different if she had not been so sexually attractive to men. It seemed to Ellen that men had always been the cause of her sorrow and pain; then again, they had made it possible for her to achieve the important things in her life.

The loss of her father and brother had left her with a void deep within. There was great anger and resentment in her. This was part of the baggage she must be rid of if she was to move on with her life. As painful as it was to be in this place, surrounded by old memories, this was where she must rid her life of the past and begin a new life.

Ellen tried listening to the preacher but all these crazy thoughts kept running through her mind. They kept coming, one after the other. She had heard that when people drown, their entire life flashes before their eyes. *Drowning,* she thought. *How stupid! I'm not drowning here in the open air!*

Like a motion picture, her life kept playing out each event in chronological order, and she was powerless to stop it. The thought of having to relive the events of her father's death and burial seemed more than she could bear.

Ellen had loved her father dearly. To have him suddenly removed from her life had been traumatic. He had been the only stability in her life and to have him suddenly taken from her left her without foundation to build on or a direction for her life. Her mother meant well, but lacked the strength of character her father possessed.

Her father's death had been an accident. He had died while hauling moonshine out of the mountains of East Tennessee. The two words best describing this period in history were Depression and Prohibition. The mountain people of East Tennessee had little choice—they would make and sell liquid corn or starve. The moonshiners made it, the bootleggers sold it, and in Tennessee, at least, the most popular name for the brew was "White Lightnin'."

The product had to be delivered to market by young men, hardly more than boys, made famous hauling the product from the mountains to the retailers in the cities in the fastest cars they could find. To be caught making, delivering, or selling meant serving time in a federal penitentiary. The wild driving and risk-taking made heroes of those foolish enough, and brave enough, to risk their lives in fast cars on mountain roads.

Ellen sat and listened. It was like she was invisible. Ordinarily, she would have been sent from the room, but she sat and listened because everyone was too involved to notice she was there.

Jim told her mother the details of how her father had died. Ellen had seen Jim before—tall, slender, dark wavy hair, and with an overinflated ego. This was the result of too much attention from women. His lack of conscience made women easy prey. Ellen had heard he had been involved in more than one nasty scandal. Her father had always kept her out of Jim's way and never allowed her mother to be alone with him. She knew her dad trusted her, but he did not trust Jim or her mother.

As Ellen listened to Jim's account of what had happened, she was somewhat skeptical, feeling he was trying to put himself in the best light possible. He was the only witness, so they had no choice but to believe what he said.

The events leading up to the tragedy were as clear in her mind today as they were the day Jim told them. According to Jim, he was standing on the corner next to the old woolen mill with nothing to do. This was easy to believe because it was during the Depression and very few people had work, and even fewer had money for entertainment. Jim said her dad had stopped and said he was going to Cosby and asked if Jim would like to go along for the ride. He hadn't told Jim why he was going. Jim hadn't asked. Everybody knew there was only one reason to go to Cosby—moonshine. There was always the element of danger, but being bored, with no prospects of anything to do, it was easy to understand why he would go. And, the chances were good the shiners would invite them to drink.

The next part of the story Ellen doubted. As Jim told it, they left the narrow blacktop road somewhere near Cosby. On leaving the blacktop, they followed a rough dirt road for about five miles. When it became too steep and rough for the car, they parked and waited.

After they had waited about fifteen minutes, the moonshiners came out of the woods leading two mules, each loaded with several cases of pint and quart jars filled with White Lightnin'.

After inspecting the jars and testing the quality, they loaded all they felt it was safe to haul and prepared to leave. The moonshiners had two cases of quarts left. They said they would make a special price if they would take them. It would soon be dark and the moonshiners did not want to go back up the mountain this late. Jim tried to tell her dad it would overload the car and make it dangerous, but her dad said he could handle it, so they loaded the extra cases.

Darkness found them still in the mountains and going into an unexpected curve at too great a speed; her dad had lost control of the overloaded car. The car left the road, went over the bank and into the river. Jim was thrown clear, but her dad was pinned beneath the steering wheel and trapped underwater. Jim tried to remove her dad from the wreck, but was not able to free him. He knew her father was dead, but walked two miles back to a store to get help.

When the car was pulled from the water, Jim was charged with transporting moonshine and was facing a long term in a federal penitentiary. Ellen could still remember her mother's exact words: "Most men would have run, but Jim stayed and did what he could, so I owe him."

Ellen remembered the hum of the overhead fans in the hall of the Sevier County courthouse. It was a hot summer day. The breeze from the fans was all that made it bearable. She thought how nice it would be if she could feel a breeze in this hot cemetery.

She had sat on that hard bench as flies zoomed in and out the open windows and listened as Jim's attorney explained to her mother, to Jim, and to one of Jim's brothers, what was taking place. The district attorney was scheduled to present charges against Jim to the grand jury within the hour.

Jim's attorney had been in a conference with the district attorney and explained to him that Ellen's mother would take the stand and swear that Jim was not involved in transporting moonshine, but was simply a hitchhiker. The district attorney said her testimony would be weak if they went to trial, but it did give him reason not to present the case to the grand jury.

The district attorney indicated to Jim's attorney that he would consider not presenting the case, but first he must get the approval of the presiding judge. Jim's attorney had then made things very clear.

He simply said, "I have told you my fee will be five hundred dollars if we do not go to trial, and one thousand dollars if we do go to trial. You must remember that there can be no guarantees."

Though his next statement was vague, even Ellen knew what he meant.

"If you can come up with fifteen hundred dollars we can walk out of here."

Within the hour, they were headed back to Knoxville, and two wallets in Sevier County were a little fatter. Fifteen hundred dollars during the Depression was a lot of money, but Jim's family got the money somewhere. She understood it wasn't the first time they bought him out of trouble, and it wouldn't be the last.

Ellen wanted to stop her memories here and now, but she was powerless to do so. By now she was convinced she could never be rid of all this garbage and free to start a new life until she had it all neatly packaged and buried here with her husband.

Ellen knew what was coming next even before it flashed through her mind's eye. She remembered the words of her mother: "Jim stayed with him when most men would have run, and I owe him."

She could not help wondering if her mother would have felt so obligated if it had been someone else and not a womanizer like Jim.

Jim seemed to feel he, in turn, owed her mother and spent the next year trying to help ease her through her period of bereavement. He was with her day and night. Ellen remembered the nights they spent in her mother's bedroom, and the sound of the radio as Gene Autry sang "Back in the Saddle Again." She was only fifteen, but she knew Autry was not the only one back in the saddle. This was a part of the resentment she still felt, because she had needed her mother more that year than during any other time in her life. This affair ran its course within the year. As soon as Jim got back on his feet, he was out hunting for younger stuff.

Jim's being out of the picture had not improved things for Ellen, because it left her mother a very unhappy person. Ellen promised herself that she would never let any man use her in this way.

It was Brad's belief that this was the basic cause of her unhappiness. She had used those hazel eyes, blonde hair, and voluptuous curves to get everything men could give her, but had failed to find what her heart truly wanted. Ellen, at this point, wasn't sure what she wanted, but was certain there had to be something more to life than she had experienced.

He had explained to her that she felt she had used the men in her life to realize her own ambitions and, because of this feeling, she regarded herself as nothing more than a whore. Reliving the past would give her a more realistic and objective view and enable her to see herself for the person she truly is. Ellen felt it might be working, but was it worth all the pain?

Suddenly the roar of an engine and the squeal of tires on the blacktop just outside the cemetery gate made her heart jump. Ellen realized she was about to be bombarded by memories she had hoped would not come.

Her father was not a regular on the moonshine run; he only did it part-time. Most people had wondered why he did it at all, but she knew, and it had only made his death harder to bear.

She remembered the day the letter came from Little Skip. She listened with her ear to the parlor door as her father read it to her mother. Her heart sank to the floor as he read the words, "Bruce is breaking down fast. If you don't buy his way out of here soon, it will be too late."

Bruce was her older brother, her hero, and her father's only son. She was not jealous because she knew her father loved her, but Bruce was his life.

Her father had been working every job he could find, trying to get enough money to bribe someone to get Bruce out of the federal penitentiary. After receiving Little Skip's letter, he turned to the only source of fast income available. It had cost him his life.

Bruce and Little Skip had been among the first of the drivers on those mountain roads. Her dad tried his best to stop Bruce from becoming involved with Little Skip, but he had not been successful.

Little Skip went by that name because his father was known as Big Skip. She had no idea where the odd name came from, but it suited them because they were odd people. Big Skip sold moonshine retail and spent most of every day standing on the corner in front of his house waiting for customers. The police never found out where he kept it hidden, or else he had paid them well.

Her mother warned her at an early age not to go near the old man; when she was older she understood why. She had heard Bruce and Little Skip talk about how Big Skip gave little girls money so he could feel them up. In later years, she wondered why someone hadn't reported him.

Little Skip was a much better person than his father. He idolized Bruce. Her father had objected to the friendship between them; he knew it would lead to trouble, but there wasn't anything he could do to change it.

They started hauling moonshine in an old Model-T Ford bought with money Little Skip borrowed from his father. They paid the money back by hauling him moonshine from Cosby and for others at the same time.

Their business was an instant success. People liked Little Skip but, more importantly, they trusted Bruce. As long as Bruce was involved, they knew the product would be the best grade and never watered down. They had several friends who were also hauling and they soon formed a tight-knit and very loyal clan. These young knights of "Thunder Road" soon became heroes to both the mountain girls and the city girls.

This mixture of fame and newfound wealth soon led them to believe they were invincible. Their exalted status reached a new level when they replaced their Model T with the new 1929 Ford Model A. These ragtops, with the half-door split windshield, were the ultimate in the moonshine hauling business. They immediately had their friends who worked in the marble mills take the engine heads, put them on the rub bed, and polish them down. This made the head thinner and increased the horsepower. In the trade, they were referred to as "hotheads."

Because of the increased compression, these new hotheads had a tendency to blow the skirt off pistons. This did not pose a problem because, with a good supply of pistons on hand and a good shade tree, they could have a car back on the road in no time.

Ellen still knew many of these so-called "mechanics." They were now keeping the cars running on the dirt tracks beginning to open up in Tennessee, Georgia, and North Carolina. They now had the equipment to outrun the law anywhere at any time. A favorite trick was to unload the moonshine and then hang around until the police showed up. Then a chase through the neighborhood would take place with the police always losing. With the door of the driver's side tied forward to the side of the hood, they would drive with one foot on the running board. This added to their status as local heroes, but only served to infuriate the police.

Her father had cautioned Bruce, "Make enough enemies and one day they will bring you down."

The new cars added quickly to their wealth and fame because they opened up the speakeasy trade to the north.

Their new customers brought them in contact with a new kind of criminal, or at least they were different from the mountain people they knew. They now became a part of the high rollers and tried to follow their lead. They imported party girls and combined sex and moonshine, trying to bring the speakeasy concept to the South. They had forgotten they were a part of the Bible Belt. The locals looked at the girls not as party girls but as whores. This venture didn't last long because the authorities, pressured by the electorate, moved in fast and closed the cat houses.

Her father had been heartbroken because Bruce had taken part in such a venture. He had been near tears when he told Bruce, "Running moonshine is against man's law, but this is against the law of God."

Ellen felt Bruce was not in favor of the way things were going, but greed had taken over and was driving the group in a mad effort to acquire more and more wealth.

Counterfeit money was to be their fatal mistake. When they found out moonshine would bring ten times the price if they took bad money, the temptation proved to be too great. Unlike in the north, merchants in small towns in the south remembered easily who had given them tens and twenties, so the federal agents tracked them down easily.

It still caused Ellen pain remembering the agony her father suffered when Bruce was convicted. Bruce and Little Skip had both been sent to the federal penitentiary and Little Skip's letter telling how Bruce was being affected had cost her father his life.

Bruce wasn't allowed to come home for his father's funeral, but they did bring him by the house to view his father's body. He was brought in dragging the leg iron and the two guards never left his side. As they turned from the casket and led him toward the door, Ellen moved forward and the guards seemed ready to stop her, but then moved back. She kissed his cheek and looked into his eyes, seeing deep pools of remorse. She knew that she would never see Bruce again in this life. He had lost all will to live.

Bruce died within the year. Little Skip said he was stir-crazy. Little Skip was released a few years later. When Ellen saw him, he was wandering the streets in a world of his own. He never shaved and talked constantly to himself, to Bruce, and to others who were no longer there. If this was what he had meant when he wrote that Bruce was stir-crazy, then Ellen felt it was a blessing that Bruce had died in prison.

Chapter II

Ellen pulled herself back to reality; she was sure the preacher must be through by now. He wasn't. He was still praying. All those memories had flooded back in a matter of seconds. How much more could she stand—this was all too painful! Her psychiatrist had said it would not be easy. He had insisted this was the only way and the only place to rid herself of her past.

Ellen looked toward the preacher, and then let her eyes rest for a moment on the casket. She dropped her eyes again. They came to rest on her mother's foot marker. This brought back more painful memories.

During that period of her life, everyone had either died or walked away. There were only the two of them, Ellen and her mother, and they were on their own. Her mother had taken the only path open to her. To survive, she sold the devil's brew that had taken the life of her husband and her son. Ellen did not feel that the next few years were the worst years of her life, but they certainly were not as good as those spent with her father and Bruce.

The threat of being caught by the police had been hard on her mother's nerves. It was a constant pressure and could wear anyone down. Some police could be bought with money, others with the favors only a woman could give. Ellen was in her late teens and more than one of the city's cops had made a move on her. From the very beginning, she had let them know she did not intend to buy protection with her body and most had backed off. Her mother was aware of what was taking place and was constantly on guard.

One of the more aggressive officers had come in one day when her mother was gone to the corner grocery. Ellen was pouring him a drink when he slipped his arm around her waist and cupped one of her breasts with the other hand. She was struggling to get free when her mother walked in. He released her immediately, but not before her mother saw what was taking place. She sent Ellen from the room, but Ellen stayed close to the door so she could hear what was said. Her mother came straight to the point, letting the officer know that, if he wanted that kind of favor, it would have to come from her. And, if she ever caught him trying that with her daughter again, she would cut off what little he had and feed it to him. After that incident, Ellen was never bothered again.

There were some funny things that happened during those teenage years. One of the funniest started running through her mind, and she almost laughed; she hoped no one saw her smile. It happened to one of the fattest cops on the city's police force.

The railroad bank across the street was covered with honeysuckle and provided the perfect hiding place for an excess stock of moonshine. Occasionally the police would hunt through that honeysuckle like kids hunting for Easter eggs. Ellen never did decide if they did it just to impress the public or if someone had failed to pay off.

On this occasion, the fat cop was giving the honeysuckle a real stomping and working up a sweat. Coming down the hill toward the bridge that spanned the railroad tracks was a farmer driving a Ford Model T truck. About halfway down the hill that Model T lost a wheel. Ellen learned something that day—when a car loses a wheel, the wheel picks up speed and outruns the car. That wheel came tearing down the hill straight for him. He looked up and saw the wheel coming. Right then she also learned something else—fat men can run; all they need is the proper motivation. That fat cop must have set a new world record for the fifty-yard dash through honeysuckle.

The teenage boys had a story they loved to tell about him. Ellen wasn't sure if it really happened or was just something they had concocted to get attention but, true or not, it was still a wild tale and always good for a laugh. One of the neighborhood women had agreed to take care of his needs. They knew what was about to take place, so they positioned themselves outside the bedroom window to watch. According to them, they watched for at least five minutes as the big boy tried to get some position where he could make contact. He struggled with it, but his belly was always in the way, or his penis was just too short. Suddenly he got up. They thought he was giving up. Instead, he picked her up and carried her into the kitchen, sat her on the table, and walked up to it. Where there's a will, there's a way!

Ellen could say one thing about those years when her mother sold White Lightnin'—they were not boring. Today, the things that entertained her then would probably sound crude, but she still remembered the day when old Madge earned the title of "The Hottest Tail in Little Cosby." Madge weighed about 250 pounds, could drink her weight in liquid corn and still remain on her feet. She could also out-cuss anyone, and it took very little to set her off.

On this particular day, Madge was loaded to the gills. Some of the neighbors had made her mad and, though she was probably too drunk to remember any details, she was still determined to express what she felt about them. Madge removed her drawers, painted both cheeks of her fat ass with rouge, and stuck it out the window to moon her neighbors.

This didn't bother the women she was trying to insult, but rather served as entertainment and a break in the otherwise boring day. It might all have ended right there, but one of the boys in the neighborhood decided it was time for him to add his bit to the entertainment. He took his air rifle and hit the bull's eye on the first shot. He must have pumped the gun to full force for that copper-coated pellet buried at least an inch deep in her right cheek. Madge tumbled out of the window onto her bedroom floor and lay there squealing like a stuck hog. The women came to her rescue and finally got her quieted down enough to start trying to remove the shot.

Ellen's mother started the operation by trying to remove it with a darning needle, while Madge cussed and screamed. This did not work, so the women finally had to slit the skin about one-half inch with a razor blade so they would have room to reach it with tweezers. The operation now complete, they decided something must be done to ward off infection. There wasn't a bottle of alcohol to be found, so they decided on the next best thing, White Lightnin'. When that White Lightnin' hit the open wound, Madge found some new words the neighbors had never heard. Her screams carried for miles.

She then started yelling, "It's on fire, it's burning, pour water on it."

And so it was that Madge earned the title of "The Hottest Tail in Little Cosby."

Things might have quieted down and been forgotten, but the kids found out Madge was quite sensitive about the situation and that was all they needed. Madge would be walking down the street, and some boy would yell, "It's burning."

And old Madge would start cussin'. It reached the place that even yelling the word "water" would set her off, but it was advisable to run for your life if you asked the question, "Madge, what's the price, now that you are having a fire sale?"

Although the police were never overly aggressive, they did raid frequently to let the public know they were on the job. The house they rented had a fireplace with an iron grate to heat it. The fireplace had a brick mantle and the wall was brick three feet on each side of the fireplace. Her mother had designed this fireplace and had a friend construct it. One brick was left loose; behind that brick was a metal box just large enough for a pint bottle. This was in her mother's bedroom and, when she went in to pour a shot for a customer, she always closed the door. This hiding place served them well and was never discovered.

On one occasion, her mother came very close to getting caught. Ellen had been standing at the cook stove making gravy for their supper when her mother was handing a six-ounce bottle to a customer at the back door. Her mother was always very suspicious and on this occasion it paid off—it was a set up! Ellen's mother spotted the police coming around the corner and reacted quickly. She pulled the cork on the bottle and poured six ounces of White Lightnin' in the gravy. It was a miracle that none was spilled on the stove causing a fire. Heat evaporates alcohol very rapidly, so the police were left without evidence.

Because it was a setup, a reporter for the local paper was along to write a story, but his story was lost along with the evidence. Being a good reporter, he found another story of even greater interest. His recipe for moonshine gravy that appeared in the evening news brought Ellen a lot of attention at school.

Selling moonshine was not an easy job. Some customers came by early in the morning for a shot before going to work; others came by late at night for a bottle to help them sleep. Ellen's mother would not let her handle the product on a regular basis, so her mother got very little rest.

The winter Ellen turned eighteen her mother began to break. The strain and stress were wearing her down. She made it through the winter and the next summer by sheer willpower. In November, just two days after Ellen's nineteenth birthday, her mother died of influenza.

The snow was blowing when they buried her mother and it had to have been the most miserable day of Ellen's life. For the first time, Ellen was alone in the world. Not a single member of her family was left to share her grief or her future. As Ellen contemplated that future, she felt lost, lonely, and afraid.

Chapter III

Many of the other moonshine dealers were present at her mother's funeral. Ellen knew they would do all they could to protect one of their own, but no amount of help would make her sell moonshine. The police did not want money from her for protection—they could get money from the others. What they wanted from her others did have, but it wasn't packaged as appealingly. Standing before her mother's grave, Ellen promised herself that she would find a way to survive without using her body to buy protection.

Sitting by the fire that night as a storm raged outside, Ellen read her mother's journal and realized her mother was smarter than she had thought.

> *Dearest Ellen,*
>
> *We both know you will never be able to sell moonshine—the price would be too great. Realizing you would need some money to tide you over, I have been laying back all that I could. You will find the bank book in the back of the top chest drawer. Your name is on it so you will have no trouble. I had hoped to have enough for you to get advanced schooling, but that isn't going to happen. I don't feel I can make it through the winter, but if you are careful, there is maybe enough for you to hold on until you can find a way out.*

Ellen knew what her mother meant. She had not been able to better her own situation, but she did want more for her daughter. Ellen had cried more than once for Bruce and her father, but that night she shed what seemed like a bucket of tears for her mother.

Why she had never cried before for her mother, she could not understand. She was a woman and should have been able to see the price that life demanded of another woman. That night, for the first time, she blamed Bruce for all the suffering and heartache her family had endured. His foolishness had contributed indirectly to the death of both her father and mother. Her father's life had ended instantly; her mother's was drawn out and more painful. Ellen decided that she was not going to be the next victim of her brother's folly.

Ellen dried the tears from her eyes and did some simple calculations. Her mother had been able to give her no more than six months to find a way to survive on her own, so by July she must find an answer to her dilemma. That night, she tossed and turned looking for a solution, but none was apparent. Even as the sun brightened up her room, her future was still just as dark.

Suddenly Ellen was startled by a knock at the door. She could not believe some drunk—unaware of her mother's death—was after an early-morning drink. She slipped into her robe and headed for the door, ready to give someone a good cussing.

Ellen was surprised to find it wasn't a customer, but Wesley, her next-door neighbor. Wes had been very helpful the last few days, giving advice, even driving her to the funeral home and helping her with the preparations for her mother's funeral. He had always been a good neighbor. As Ellen's mother had always said, "We have enough enemies, so we must take care of each other."

Wes stood there grinning and said, "I am here to take you to breakfast. I think you need to get away from the house for a while so you can examine your situation and make some decisions." Wes was the kind of person who felt you should make all decisions immediately, never sleep until all work is done and tomorrow's work planned.

Wes went back to his house while she pulled herself together. It was hard for Ellen to do much with red, swollen eyes, caused by crying and lack of sleep, but once she was ready, they walked across the bridge to Betty's Café for breakfast.

Ellen did not realize how hungry she was until Betty brought her a large platter of ham and eggs. She tried to remember when she had eaten last but did not have any idea. She hoped Wes would not think she ate like this all the time.

When they finished eating, they sat and drank coffee, and talked about Ellen's problems and what she must do in a very short time. Ellen did most of the talking, and Wes did the listening, but she did little more than relate her problems because the solutions were not readily available.

The next three months they spent many mornings together having breakfast and talking. Most days Wes went back to work. Ellen spent the day looking for work. Wes discouraged her from taking a job in an all-night drive-in; it was too dangerous. She could have made good money as a carhop, but she did not have transportation, so working late into the morning was not practical. The more Ellen looked, the more she realized why people sold moonshine—jobs were scarce, even the least desirable ones.

When Wes could get someone to work for him, they would go to a movie. She tried to pay her own way, but Wes refused to let her. Since her mother's death, all her customers were now trading with Wes, and he felt he owed her something for the business.

It was a warm night in April. They had been sitting on her front porch. She was getting ready to go in and Wes was going home. At her door she turned to say good night. He suddenly took her in his arms and held her close; his lips met hers in a long, lingering kiss. She had seen a lot and heard even more, so she was not totally ignorant, but this was a new experience for Ellen. She stayed in his arms for a moment, not knowing what to do; then she gently pulled free, stepped inside, and closed the door. She leaned back against the closed door as her body continued to respond to feelings that were new to her. The feelings were warm and pleasant, but she also felt confused. She did not understand what she was feeling or why.

Ellen slept little that night. She was sure that her life was about to change. Wes, up until now, had been a good and trusted friend, but she knew that things between them would be different. She had no way of knowing his intention. He had never said he loved her, and he had never made advances such as she had experienced from other men.

Had she said or done anything that might have caused Wes to think that she wanted him to kiss her? Had he fallen in love with her? She must see Wes again but dreaded it. She did not feel love for him, and yet he had become a part of her life. She had come to depend on Wes. The thought that she might no longer have him to lean on was frightening.

It was later than usual when Wes knocked at her door. He had also experienced a long night. They decided not to go to breakfast. They had already had coffee—she to wake up, he to sober up. Wes seemed eager to talk, and she wanted to talk also, but was at a loss as to what to say. Wes started by apologizing for what happened the night before. He had not planned to kiss her, but because of the strong feelings he had for her, it just happened. Wes told her he had always had very strong feelings for her, but because she deserved more than he could offer her, he had kept his distance. He had only wanted to ease her pain after her mother's death, but had come to love her more than he ever felt was possible. He said that he knew she deserved more than he had to offer, but if she would marry him, he would always love and protect her. Wes did not ask for an immediate answer, only that she give his proposal serious thought.

Ellen was not used to making decisions and certainly not one that would affect the rest of her life. She realized she didn't love Wes and had told him so. Wes felt that in time she would learn to love him and that was all that mattered.

Ellen needed someone to talk with. There were only two women she had ever talked with besides her mother: Jane who lived next door to Wes, and Alice who lived next to Jane. Ellen doubted that Alice knew enough about life to give any useful advice. Jane, on the other hand, had ample experience, but Ellen was not sure it made her a good counselor. Ellen had witnessed firsthand some of Jane's experience.

The neighborhood iceman was known for his many conquests. Ellen had once heard her mother say that, if he had filled as many ice boxes as he had hot boxes, he would be a millionaire. Jane numbered among his conquests. Everyone knew when Jane hung diapers on the back porch on Sunday morning, she was not behind with her laundry; it meant that the coast was clear. Her husband had gone to church with the children, and—"the iceman cometh!" That play on words always brought a chuckle when the women gossiped.

These two women were her only choice. After a week of soul-searching, Ellen went to them for advice. As she expected, Jane did most of the talking. Ellen told them she was not in love with Wes, but she did like him.

Jane replied, "It is much better to be married to someone you like but do not love than to be married to someone you love but do not like." She then quickly added, "But, neither will work if the sex isn't good."

Ellen did not understand either statement, and they had little effect on her decision. Ellen in later years came to understand how profound both statements had been.

Chapter IV

Ellen and Wes were married two weeks after his proposal. She did not like to admit it, but it was a marriage of convenience. She had no other choice.

Wes was able to get help with his business so they could go to Florida on a two-week honeymoon. Ellen had never been on a train before and that trip greatly influenced the rest of her life.

Wes had a private compartment for them. If good sex was as important as Jane said, then this marriage would be a great success. After that first trip, the sound of a train whistle was all it took to turn Ellen on. To her it became a bugle call for foreplay. In the first year of the marriage, Wes often joked, "If the trains don't quit blowing for the crossing just below our house, I will never live to be an old man."

Whenever possible, if Ellen had to travel, she insisted it be by train. There was something about the sound of the train wheels rolling along the rails that made every trip a new honeymoon.

The men who later on became a part of Ellen's life often wondered why she insisted on traveling by train. After their first trip, they no longer cared why. They would have been willing to take a train on a burning trestle over hell, just as long as Ellen was in their bunk!

Ellen had never seen the ocean, but then she had never seen anything outside her own neighborhood. They walked the beach at night and made love under the stars. Wes always slept late. Ellen took long walks on the deserted beach early in the morning.

She had never known such peace and contentment equal to that she experienced as she walked barefoot through the sand. Ellen listened to the gentle splash of the waves along the shore and marveled at the calm it brought to her inner spirit. It was her dream that some day she would be able to take advantage of this experience whenever she needed to quiet the inner turmoil she so often felt. The two weeks of their honeymoon were at that time the most wonderful time of her life. It was followed by another exciting train ride home.

When they arrived home, Wes became involved again in his business. Ellen tried to adjust to her new life by making their home a place where they could relax together. Wes had to work all hours. For Ellen, this was the kind of life she was used to. It was the same way her mother had worked and all the bootleggers did the same.

Ellen knew what was to be expected. She did all she could to help him relax when he was off. They tried to get away for a movie at least once a week. They were able to have breakfast at Betty's nearly every morning. Aside from an occasional visit to talk with Jane and Alice, Ellen spent her time reading. This wasn't a very exciting life but Ellen was happy because it was all she had ever known.

Wes seldom went anywhere without her, except once a month he went to the cockfights and was gone all night.

Most sellers of moonshine kept fighting roosters in their backyard. Wes was no exception. Each rooster was kept in a separate pen. Ellen kept water and food for each one as well as cleaned each pen.

It was the nature of these birds to fight. If two got out of their cage at the same time, a fight always occurred. They would fight until one became totally exhausted. Ellen knew they couldn't hurt each other; their spurs had been trimmed with only a small stub remaining.

Ellen didn't know anything about cockfighting. Thinking this was all there was to it, she never asked questions.

She might never have known any different had she not become attached to one of the more beautiful birds. Ellen asked where her favorite bird was when Wes returned one morning without him. Wes said he lost. Ellen continued to ask questions and that's when she learned the truth. She cringed as he told her how curved razor-sharp blades were attached to those trimmed spurs and the birds fought until one was dead.

Even now, at her husband's grave, she felt nauseated by that memory. That morning, when he told her, she had gone outside and lost her breakfast. Their first fight followed and Ellen was very vocal as she expressed her opinion of men so barbaric who could treat those beautiful birds in such a cruel manner. Protest as much as she might, horse racing might be the sport of kings, but cockfighting was the sport of the moonshine kings.

They hardly spoke for a whole week, but Wes refused to give up his sport. This episode was the beginning of the end of their marriage.

Wes was a good person at heart, but other character flaws began to show. They had probably been there, but only after that one incident had she started looking at Wes with a critical eye. She was having doubts about her marriage.

Wes started staying out at night. Ellen could see signs it wasn't always his sport—there were other women involved. Had she loved Wes, it might have been different, but she hadn't learned to love him. In many ways she had started to dislike him. Ellen had also come to understand that liking someone and having a good sexual relationship is not enough. Men and women alike, to be secure in a relationship, must know they are loved.

Her marriage was over, but she was in no position to move on. She was trapped and she knew it; she was back to square one. Things in her life were just as they were when she married Wes, but now there was no one to come to her aid. She had married Wes because she had no other choice, but now there simply was no choice to be made, right or wrong.

Their marriage continued to get worse. There were no arguments; rather it was simply a situation where both of them went through the motions. Wes worked. She cooked, cleaned house, and made it one day at a time.

On a very hot summer night they were sitting on the porch trying to find a cool spot. They were getting on each other's nerves. In desperation, they decided to take a walk. When they got to the corner and started up the hill, they realized the Holiness worshippers had erected a tent on the lot next to the store and were having a revival. This happened each summer about the same time. They had been told it could be very entertaining, but they had never attended.

When they got across the street from the tent, they saw a crowd outside the tent and along the sidewalk watching the service. They decided to join them.

Ellen had never seen anything like this before. Along with the singing, praying, and shouting, there were those who would start jerking and shaking like they had lost all control.

There were also those who spoke in tongues. After she had listened for a while, Ellen began to wonder if the Lord even knew what they were saying.

A man standing in front of them remarked, "I wish the little preacher would hurry up and start." Then he started telling the man next to him about the team of preachers who were conducting the revival. "That's old Tall Tom out there now, but you just wait, when that short preacher gets in the act, things will begin to heat up."

They did not have long to wait. A small fellow about five feet five started praying and shouting. Things reached a fever pitch. The shaking and gyrating became more ecstatic. Ellen didn't think things could get any wilder, but then the preacher started walking the two-by-four altar rail speaking in unknown tongues.

He chanted, "Hondi, hondi, chicki, my hondi."

The crowd went wild. They responded to his every word and motion. Ellen thought, *How ridiculous.* She glanced at Wes. He was totally captivated.

They returned to the services the next two nights. Ellen was amazed when she realized that Wes was really becoming emotionally involved. On the third night, Wes answered the altar call, and for the rest of the night was very quiet and seemed to be in deep thought.

On the following day, the short preacher came to visit Wes. After much praying and counseling, Wes was filled with the Holy Spirit. Ellen wasn't sure what the Holy Spirit was, but it didn't seem to do him any harm.

Ellen and Wes continued to attend the services, but she did not participate. The minister continued to come by the house, but Ellen was not fooled. She knew—his interest in her was physical and not spiritual. Wes gave up selling whiskey and took up preaching. Ellen decided the reverend's interest could be a solution to her problem.

It was Friday morning. The revival team was scheduled to leave town after the Sunday services. Ellen was beginning to wonder if she had read some signals wrong. Wes was out in the community with Tall Tom witnessing to his friends and neighbors. He had made his decision: no more selling the devil's brew, the rest of his life would be dedicated to saving souls.

The reverend was late. Finally, Ellen saw him coming from the alley and she headed for the back door to meet him.

She had already decided he would get what he wanted, but only after she was sure she would get her way out of here and a new start in life. Whatever it took, she would not go down a dead-end street, as she had with Wes.

He introduced himself for the first time: Jeremy K. Grimes.

Jeremy had more than one surprise for Ellen: the first being that he was leaving Tall Tom and Wes would take his place. Wes had not told Ellen his plan, so he apparently didn't include her as a part of it. Jeremy's next surprise came with his proposition to Ellen.

He had been called to serve as president of a new Holiness Divinity School and he wanted her to come with him as his wife. He told her a campus filled with college-aged girls was too great a temptation for him. He had been advised by a close friend that he should find a wife who could assist him in his new venture. He needed a wife who could fill his personal needs, and also be a companion who could further his career. Jeremy was very complimentary as he told her she had the necessary qualifications. She would be a great asset. It would be necessary for her to stay in a nearby town until her divorce from Wes became final. They would then be married, and she would join him in their home on campus. Ellen was shocked; this was totally unexpected. She was too smart to jump at this opportunity, but told him he would get her answer Sunday morning. If she did decide to go with him, everything would be ready for them to leave on Sunday night.

Chapter V

Ellen was ready. They left immediately after the Sunday evening service. She did not feel she owed Wes an explanation; she simply left a note telling him her lawyer would contact him. Jeremy left her with C. Conrad Clevenger, his lawyer friend who would handle her divorce. His wife's name was Dorothy, mostly known as Dot.

Jeremy told Ellen to pay close attention to what Dot would tell her. She was known as a very accomplished hostess, and what Ellen could learn would be very helpful in her future position.

Had she known the great responsibilities she was about to undertake, she might have chickened out. It was a big jump from bootlegger's wife to the wife of a college president, but Ellen was too ignorant of the ways of the world to realize it. Thinking back, Ellen doubted it would have changed her decision because there were no other answers to her problem.

Ellen suddenly became aware of what was going on around her. She was surprised to find the service still dragging on. Her life was flashing through her mind at the speed of sound, but the service seemed to move at a snail's pace.

Ellen glanced to the right across the foot of her husband's casket. She saw Dot, and another part of her life began to unfold.

There had never been any doubt in Ellen's mind that Dot had contributed more to the mature, polished individual she had become than any other person. While Dot's husband, Con, took care of her divorce, she was grooming Ellen for the life she was about to enter.

Dot, as she attended meetings, entertained friends and clients of her husband, and even as she shopped for Ellen's clothes, was grooming her to be the helper Jeremy needed. Ellen was still amazed that any person could be dominant yet humble, controlling yet gracious, so in charge while seeming to be just another person in a happy group of people. Dot's personality and know-how, plus her ability to organize, were the reasons behind her husband's great success.

Con, as Dot called her husband, was without a doubt the most complex person Ellen had ever met. He was a close friend of Jeremy. Though he was well respected and highly regarded as an estate, business, and tax lawyer, he had no close friends—at least Ellen had not met them.

Dot was his personality, social conscience, and his link to all other parts of society outside his profession. His clients knew Con to be strictly honest, and that their business ethics must be above reproach if they wanted to remain his clients. Because of Con's uncompromising honesty and his brilliance as an attorney, most of his cases were settled by arbitration. Even the judges had great respect for him; they would often confer with him when they had difficult cases.

At home, Con was an even more complex person. During the six months Ellen lived in their home, she never saw Con without a coat and tie. Dot joked that she was the only person who had ever seen Con out of uniform. She confided in Ellen that her husband was a very shy person who found it hard to function outside his profession. As long as he was carrying his briefcase and fully dressed in coat and tie, he was like a four-star general in full command, but once he had left his legal battlefield, he became fully dependent on her to take command. Ellen found that Con followed his routine even when only the three of them were in the house. If he sat down in the evening after they had dined, he might listen to his white Crosley radio or read, but he never loosened his tie.

Dot explained these peculiarities of her husband and, in so doing, told Ellen all she would learn about her future husband's past prior to their marriage.

Con, Dot, and Jeremy had been friends since they were young, growing up together in an orphanage in the mountains of East Tennessee. It was a mission school as well as an orphanage. That's where they had received their education. Because they were three gifted students, they received help in furthering their education and had each excelled in their respective fields.

Dot was a registered nurse but had worked only briefly since marrying Con. She had realized, in spite of Con's brilliance, that his shyness would make it impossible for him to succeed unless she made it possible. She had made it her mission to ensure his life would be full and productive. Con's peculiar lifestyle was really a fence he had erected around himself to conceal his extreme shyness.

He had been doing work for the church that had called Jeremy to be president of their new school. Con had been responsible for Jeremy getting the position, but Dot assured Ellen that Jeremy was fully qualified. This information was all Dot would give Ellen about her future husband; the rest of his past must come from Jeremy.

Dot continued to groom Ellen for her future role, taking great pains in her selection of Ellen's clothes. She knew she must play down Ellen's striking beauty. In her choice of outfits for Ellen, Dot was striving to use her beauty as an asset and not as a matter of concern for the other wives of the school staff.

Ellen's education started off slowly, beginning with church functions, and gradually came to include larger, more formal occasions. The wife of C. Conrad Clevenger was in great demand, because it was well-known that Dot could make any party a success. Con's name on the committee insured the success of any fund-raising event, and to have both Clevengers attend a function was a feather in the cap of the hostess. As a team, Dot and Con had few equals, and it had brought them social position and great wealth.

Ellen attended these functions and acquired a knowledge that later earned her the reputation as one of the outstanding hostesses of the academic world. She found happiness with these new friends she had never known before. Dot became Ellen's first real friend and the older sister she had always longed for.

Chapter VI

Jeremy returned just before Christmas. They were married secretly, because it was imperative that they arrive on campus as a married couple. They spent their honeymoon with Dot and Con. Ellen cherished the memory of that Christmas as the most enjoyable of her life.

The carol "Peace on Earth" had true meaning for Ellen; she felt a peace she had never known before. She was among friends, and she felt the spirit of goodwill all about her.

Ellen had worried about Jeremy. How would he receive her now that six months had passed? His first look told her what she needed to know. She knew without a doubt that he liked what he saw. As time passed, he had the look of a man pleased with himself; he had made a good choice.

Jeremy and Ellen left the day after Christmas. They wanted to be on campus and settled in before the students and other faculty members arrived. Ellen wasn't apprehensive at all. She had been trained by the very best, and knowing that Dot was only a phone call away gave her confidence.

Before faculty members and students returned to campus, Ellen and Jeremy spent some time getting to know one another.

"If the sex is good, any marriage can make it." She also started to wonder if she had been lucky with sex partners or just easily satisfied. She had thought that Wes was a good lover, but now she found him only adequate. She finally concluded that Jeremy had a sincere desire to make her happy. The belief that sex was good only if there was love was just a myth. It would be a few years before she learned that sex was even better when love was there.

Ellen still did not know about the part of Jeremy's life that Dot had said must come from him. One evening, as they sat in the library, he said there were some things she needed to know. Trembling, she sat quietly beside him on the love seat, not trusting herself to respond.

He had left the mountains with Dot and Con and traveled to Atlanta. There he went to divinity school. Con had studied law, Dot had become a nurse. He had no idea where the grant money came from, but with scholarship money, all three had received their degrees, and all three were first in their class.

Dot and Con had married and moved to Chattanooga, Tennessee, where Dot was working as a nurse and Con was working to establish a practice. Jeremy was not bragging, just stating he had become known as a dynamic evangelist.

Because of his outstanding record as a student and a hard worker, Jeremy received an offer to serve as youth director in a large church while studying for his doctorate. He continued to make a name for himself. He not only excelled in his postgraduate work, but was successful in his new job. Jeremy proved to be an outstanding organizer. This, coupled with his ability as a dynamic speaker, put a demand on his time that became a burden that would have been too much for most people. To Jeremy, it was a dream fulfilled. His dedication and zeal for winning people to Christ gave him strength that many didn't have.

Ellen listened. She was not surprised. She might have been skeptical when they first met, but after the brief time with Jeremy and his friends, she knew anything was possible where they were concerned.

Jeremy was unmoved as he related the first part about his past. However, as he continued his story, he was unable to remain detached and without feeling.

Ellen had mixed feelings about this part of the story that were hard to understand even today. She could reach but one conclusion; she would always share a place in his heart with another woman.

Ruth had been his first love and would always be a part of his life. Ellen could not help feeling great sympathy and sorrow as he related this part of his past.

Ruth had been a member of the church where Jeremy served. From the day they met, their attraction for one another could not be ignored. They fell madly in love. She was the daughter of the dean where Jeremy was studying for his doctorate. Ruth was a few years younger than him, but would graduate from college about the same time he earned his doctorate. They were planning to be married as soon as Jeremy finished his studies. Her mother and father had given their blessing to the union and were elated that their daughter would be a part of the church they served.

A young man with a doctorate in theology, first in his class, and already with a reputation for being a mover and shaker, was planning to marry a girl whose father was dean of an outstanding school of theology. A match like this just didn't happen; it had to be a part of a divine plan.

Jeremy had said the same thing in different words, "I could not have planned or dreamed anything so perfect. I found myself in love with a girl whose family was already established in the work I loved. With her knowledge, experience, and contacts, life would be perfect. On the night I received my doctorate, I had the world in the palm of my hand and then it exploded—all my hopes and dreams vanished in an instant."

There was agony in Jeremy's voice as he told the rest of the story. They had been to a party; he was the guest of honor, celebrating his new degree. They had both been drinking and, not being regular drinkers, they didn't realize Ruth should not be driving. Jeremy was in a coma for twenty-four hours. Ruth died in the crash. An autopsy was performed. Ruth was found to be in the early stages of pregnancy. This was the surprise Ruth had promised to tell him the next morning.

Ruth's parents were deeply hurt and very angry. The anger was directed at Jeremy. However, they were advised by their lawyer that Ruth had been driving and, therefore, no one else could be held responsible. The circumstances and the father's position made it necessary to keep down gossip. For this reason, Jeremy was allowed to attend the funeral with the family.

After the service, Jeremy returned to the family home with the rest of the family, but was immediately called into the study by Ruth's father. The dean told Jeremy that there wasn't any way he could take away Jeremy's degrees—they had already been awarded—but he would make sure Jeremy was never ordained in any conference of the Methodist Church. He was ordered to leave and never be seen near the premises again. This had little effect on Jeremy. He was in shock; much didn't even register until months later.

Chapter VII

For the next six months, Jeremy made his home with Dot and Con. For most of that period, Jeremy was depressed. What kept him from taking his own life was the assurance that God loved him and would forgive him. However, he could not forgive himself. He did not regret anything that had happened between Ruth and him. Their relationship was a beautiful and sacred memory.

During this time with Dot and Con, Jeremy would take long walks alone on the countryside and spend long periods in secret prayer, but it seemed that nothing could break the grip of his depression. Dot and Con found themselves powerless to do anything except wait and pray that he would work his way through it.

One morning Jeremy opened his Bible and found himself reading the story of David and Bathsheba. God had taken their son as punishment for their sins. David mourned and did penance, asking God to spare their son. In his agony, David acknowledged his sin and asked for God's forgiveness, but his son was not spared. After the child died, David gave up his mourning and self-loathing, bathed, dressed, and returned to his duties as king. Many were surprised at this change and questioned David. His reply was, "He can no longer come to me, but I can go to him."

These words penetrated the depths of Jeremy's heart. Ruth and their unborn child were lost to him, but, like David, he could go to them. The only way was through his savior as he fulfilled his calling.

That night Jeremy told Dot and Con he had decided to move on with his life and do the work he had been called to do. Only when Dot asked how he intended to go about it did he remember the dean's words to him. All avenues were closed to Jeremy. There was no chance he would ever be able to follow his calling through the church of his choice.

He was greatly disturbed by this roadblock, but he was confident that God would make it possible for him to follow his heart. He must leave it to God to provide him a new opportunity in his own time and in his own way.

Jeremy didn't wish to get far from church work. He took a job in church photography. Jeremy enjoyed this because it kept him in contact with many of the men he had met in school and through the church.

Jeremy did well for a while; then doors began to close. Friends let him know he had been blackballed from higher up, and any man who did business with him would jeopardize his own career. Jeremy learned some hard lessons. It did not take long for him to realize there are those who will rejoice at your fall, and still others who will kick a man when he is down. The most disappointing thing to Jeremy was how few people are willing to support a person or a cause if it in any way threatens their own security. Jeremy was able for a while to make a go of it by calling on other denominations where he was not known. Eventually, even there the pressure to ostracize him became so strong he was not able to fight it.

He started selling religious literature to small independent churches. His main items were hymnals, Sunday school literature, and bulletins. His orders were small—they were all small churches. The delivery time for reorder made it necessary for him to have a large customer base, and this called for extensive travel.

To cover his expenses, Jeremy found it necessary to sell Bibles door-to-door. He traveled in South Georgia for two weeks though he hardly made expenses. He was becoming discouraged and lonely.

God had let him hit the bottom and caught him on the first bounce. Tired and depressed, unable to sleep, Jeremy left a small cheap motel room and wandered aimlessly in a small southern town.

Hearing church music and with nowhere to go, he moved in the direction of the sound. On a vacant lot, a tent had been erected and a revival meeting was in progress: Holiness Church, or Holy Rollers as they were often called.

They got the name because at times the people became so emotional they would roll in the sawdust which had been spread on the bare ground. The Holy Rollers were said to resemble the Shaker denomination, shaking and jerking out of control when they became emotional. They would speak in tongues. Even the speakers didn't know what they were saying. They said it was the spirit speaking through them.

Jeremy stood outside the tent and listened. A feeling of peace and contentment flooded over him. It was like a return home after a long hard journey and every old hymn drew him nearer the group.

Jeremy had been too long outside the house of God and the fellowship of believers. The experience was bringing back memories from the past, memories of a better time and a better place.

He remembered the story of the derelict standing on the street corner listening to a Salvation Army group sing an old familiar hymn he had heard his mother sing. This flashback brought such strong emotional feelings that the man could not resist the call to return to a life he had once known. Jeremy knew this was happening to him and he was powerless to resist the desire to be a part of the body of Christ once again.

He entered the tent and took a seat on the rear makeshift pew as far in the corner as he could get. Jeremy sat there, conscious only of the praying and singing, lulled into a peaceful rest engulfed in a warm half-sleep.

He leaned forward with his head resting on the back of the pew in front of him when he heard a voice say, "Can I help you, brother?"

Looking up, Jeremy saw a tall, lanky man standing in front of him, but the rest of the tent was empty. This was how Jeremy met Tall Tom.

The floodgates opened as Jeremy told Tom what had happened to him. He let Jeremy talk though he knew most of the story. Much later, Tom would tell Jeremy he had followed his work since he was a student and he knew his great potential.

Tom knew his church had made him an outcast but had no idea what he had been doing. Jeremy filled him in on the activities and his constant failures over the last year.

Tom asked, "Have you asked God to forgive you?"

Jeremy said, "I know God has forgiven me because I know that God loves me, but I can never forgive myself, or love myself again."

Tom then reminded him of John Wesley, the founder of Methodism who, when he doubted his faith, was told by a friend, "Preach faith until you find faith."

"This is your mission." he told Jeremy. "You must preach love until you find love in every way."

"But all doors are closed to me—I have no way to tell others of God's love."

"Do what you can with what you have where you happen to be." Tom then added, "My church is open to you and there are thousands who need to hear the message of God's love."

"I can't communicate with the people I saw in the worship service and would have nothing to tell them."

Although he didn't mention the shaking and speaking in tongues, not wanting to hurt Tom's feelings, Tom still knew what he meant.

Tom then told Jeremy, "God's plan of salvation is simple, but people try to make it complicated. There are those who refuse to partake of the

Lord's Supper or serve it to Christians of other denominations. Others try to make themselves different from other Christians by declaring themselves born-again. Even a poorly educated man like me knows that all Christians are born-again in the spirit of Christ. Then there are those who think more water will wash away their sins, when even the people you saw here tonight know only the blood of Christ is needed.

"There was a time when the catchword was 'sanctified.' I know you are a Christian, brother, but have you been sanctified? Jeremy, there will always be catchwords and phrases as people try to set themselves apart as something more than sinners saved by grace. Where I stand, the speaking in tongues, shaking—even the rolling in the sawdust, if it comes to that—are nothing more than gimmicks that get the attention of people who need to know the message of God's love. This may seem strange to some people but it is no stranger than a church body who considers its leaders infallible. Grace is the important word because we are all sinners saved by grace.

"Jeremy, you are much better educated than I am, so taking the message to the people I serve will be more difficult for you, but you do have the message they need to hear. You have the ability, but beyond that, you have a gift that few people have and God expects you to use it. These people could never understand theology the way you grasp it, but they can understand God loves them. This message you have received firsthand because it is a part of your experience. I say you can do it, but only if you believe God loves these people as much as he loves any person he has created and that he wants you to deliver that message in any way and by any means possible.

"God has forgiven you, Jeremy, because he loves you. You also know the rest of that message—because God loves you, you must love others and also love yourself. The hardest part you have recognized, but preach love long enough, and one day you will love yourself."

Jeremy suddenly realized that a man short on formal education, but long on love and understanding of God's will, had opened a door for him in a way that left him no choice but to enter.

Ellen broke in on his story and asked, "How could you? It was only a show, speaking in tongues walking that altar rail."

"I had already walked on the mountaintops and needed humbling. By the first time you saw me, I had reached the point Tom had reached years before. The only thing of importance was telling these people that God loves you and I would have turned cartwheels the length of that altar rail if it were the only way."

It was at this time that Jeremy received Con's letter telling him about the opportunity now open to him. It was Con who also advised him not to attempt such an assignment as a single person but to find himself a suitable wife.

Jeremy told Ellen that he knew when he read Con's letter, God had picked her. It was her calling, the same as his.

Ellen objected, "You know I am not a Christian. I have never professed to be a follower of Christ."

"You are. You just don't know it yet."

Ellen would remember those words many times in the coming years and wonder if they were true—and, if they were, when would she know for sure?

In the few days after this morning of soul-searching, they tried to prepare themselves for the coming storm that would erupt once school resumed. It would be dinners, chapel sessions, and an opportunity for everyone to meet the new president and his wife and, of course, pass judgment. Jeremy was not the least apprehensive—he was very experienced in handling formal occasions. But for her, it caused some sleepless nights.

Chapter VIII

Ellen needed someone to talk with, so she called Dot. Dot told her not to worry; Jeremy had been picked by H.T., the power behind the throne. This was the first time Ellen heard about Henry Thomas Thompson. He was a very wealthy client of Con, a devout Christian, and a hard worker in the Holiness Church. He believed that the church must break from some of its own traditions. He wanted to educate its ministers and become a church that opened its doors to a wider following.

When Con told H.T. about Jeremy, he was willing to hire him without even meeting him. H.T. had such confidence in Con that anyone he recommended was good enough for him.

Ellen met H.T. the first week after school reconvened and it changed her life forever. He was always there when Jeremy needed him, which wasn't often, because Jeremy knew what he had to do, and did it. For Ellen, it was different. H.T. suggested people for her to call when she needed help with large college functions. Ellen called them, never knowing until years later that H.T. had called first.

Ellen's "events," as they came to be known, were the talk everywhere. Every caterer sent only his best; no one would do otherwise after H.T. had called. The other women on campus treated her with respect. Women who were known to be shrews, gossips, and backbiters, didn't dare to attack Ellen. That would put their husbands' careers in jeopardy. H.T. had money enough to get people's undivided attention.

Ellen's desire to please and make others feel at ease made her an instant success. Jeremy went to work with his usual enthusiasm, recruiting students and professors, keeping the school's needs in mind. If he were to produce the kind of ministers that H.T. wanted for the church, he must have professors with a solid background in theology. This alone, though, would not be enough. They must also be able to deliver their message and to teach.

By June, when the regular school year ended, everything was in place for the coming year to move them toward their goal. H.T. came over to discuss some plans with Ellen and Jeremy. It was at this time that Ellen found out why H.T. was such a success in business.

He started by telling Jeremy how pleased he was with the academic plans he had set in motion at the school. The next phase of their plan was to make sure the church would embrace the school as part of their ministry; otherwise it would not be a success. He wanted to move the church into the twentieth century with as little kicking and screaming as possible.

Jeremy and Ellen would go as a team to sell the school to the churches. If they were successful, the churches would not only support the school but also the pastors it sent them.

H.T. told Jeremy, "We want the people to contribute to the school because, where their money is, their heart will be also, and then it becomes their school."

He had plans mapped out for Jeremy and Ellen to travel to as many major church meetings as possible, and he would arrange for Jeremy to be the main speaker at these events.

H.T. wanted Jeremy to convince the people they now had a school they could be proud of and that it was God's plan for their church. Ellen's part was to let the wives and other women see that Dr. Jeremy Grimes had a wife who supported his work, and that God wanted all wives and mothers to be active because the school was for their children.

When H.T. said they would be gone for the entire three months, Ellen thought she would faint, but H.T. quickly brought forth his next surprise. He owned a private railcar—they would have it for the complete summer! He also had a personal servant who would travel with them and see to all their needs. H.T. would be in Europe for the summer on business, so he did not need it.

When traveling, the servant, Rufus, cooked for them in the car. Rufus had his own room in the opposite end of the car from Ellen and Jeremy, so they would have complete privacy. H.T. told them they would be in some places for several days and could spend those days and nights in a hotel. Jeremy and Ellen were speechless. This was beyond any wealth they had ever imagined.

Ellen tried to pack as lightly as possible. Jeremy told her they would probably need to buy additional clothing before the summer was over. Again, they had underestimated the accommodations in store for them. Their private quarters were large enough to accommodate all the clothes Ellen and Jeremy owned. They had their own stateroom, complete with bath and dressing area. Just outside the stateroom, Jeremy had an office comparable to his study at home. There were two seats on each side of the car where they could sit and read or just look out the window. There were pull-down tables on both sides that could be used for eating or playing cards.

During the day, when they were at meetings, Rufus cleaned the car, got laundry and dry-cleaning done, and bought supplies for the kitchen. Rufus also assured them he would have ample time to take care of any personal errands for them during the day. He also asked about their favorite foods; he was an outstanding chef.

When they finally got under way, Jeremy read their itinerary. They were hopscotching all over the country, often backtracking to pick up meetings as they were scheduled. Their only responsibility was to be on board when it was time for the train to leave.

They planned to spend most of their time in the car, but found this was not possible. In places where they spent a few days, they received invitations from friends of H.T. to spend time at their estates. They accepted graciously, and quite often found living quarters far more elaborate than they had expected. There were times they stayed in a guesthouse with a full complement of servants. In places where they had shorter stays, their hosts insisted that they attend formal functions at their country club and would invite hundreds of people to meet the dynamic young preacher with the stunning blonde wife.

The newspapers covered these events, stressing the point they were Dr. Jeremy Grimes and his wife Ellen, friends and co-workers of the capitalist Henry T. Thompson.

Jeremy had some experience in social events, but not on this scale. For Ellen, it was an entirely different world. She had never thought about the advantage her outstanding beauty gave her, but on these occasions, feeling less than adequate, she was thankful for it.

They had meetings in most of the larger cities in the Southeast. Ellen especially enjoyed the time they spent in Florida, because it gave her an opportunity to walk in the damp sand in the early morning and enjoy the sounds of the ocean and their calming effect.

The time in Atlanta would have been enjoyable for Ellen, but she felt the sorrow Jeremy was experiencing when he visited again those places he and Ruth enjoyed together.

It was on this trip that Ellen first remembered Con's advice to Jeremy not to do this without a wife. They were staying on a large estate outside Memphis, Tennessee. The couple was several years older than Jeremy and had two very attractive daughters. They were swimming in the pool just outside the guesthouse, when the two girls joined them.

Ellen, tired of swimming, told Jeremy she was going to get things ready for the meeting early the next morning. As she was leaving, Ellen had a strange feeling Jeremy didn't wish to be left alone with the girls, but she felt it was probably because they were younger and he didn't feel at ease trying to find suitable conversation.

On reaching the upstairs bedroom, Ellen walked to the window to pull down the shade. On glancing out, she saw the young girl going inside and already halfway to the main house. The older girl, probably about twenty-five, was well-stacked and about two inches shorter than Jeremy.

Ellen started to move back into the room when she saw the girl ask Jeremy to do something for her. When the girl turned her back to Jeremy, Ellen realized she was asking Jeremy to tie her bikini top. Put in this position, Jeremy had no choice but to do what the girl had asked. Ellen watched in amazement as Jeremy started to tie the bikini top. The girl released the tie on the bikini bottom and turning, shed both parts. She stood there with arms widespread, giving Jeremy a full front view at very close range. Jeremy was stunned! He looked like a deer trapped in the headlights of an approaching car.

The girl placed both arms across his shoulders, pulled herself forward, pressing her breasts against Jeremy's bare chest. This seemed to bring Jeremy back to reality. He suddenly placed a hand on the girl's shoulders and pushed her backwards into the pool. Ellen could hear Jeremy's angry words, "Now that you are cooled off, get yourself dressed, and get back to the house, and if this ever happens again, I'll tell your mother."

Jeremy turned and started back to the guesthouse as the girl put on her robe, placed both pieces of the bikini in one pocket, and headed for the house.

Ellen moved away from the window. She didn't want Jeremy to know what she had seen and heard. Ellen had already removed her own bathing suit and was wrapped in a bath towel. As Jeremy entered the room, Ellen shed her bath towel, did her own bit of seductive work, and made sure he would never regret pushing that slut into the swimming pool.

Their sex had never been better. As she lay relaxed in Jeremy's arms, Ellen was reflecting on what had led up to this. Their marriage had been one of convenience for her and one of necessity for Jeremy—could it be it had gradually become something more? Ellen could not remember Jeremy saying the words "I love you," but in every act and in every way he was saying it. Ellen was not clear about her own feelings—was she beginning to love him, or could her action be the primal instincts of a female holding on to what was hers? Ellen decided not to try to answer immediately but to enjoy the moment and leave that question for another day. No matter what, if it was truly love or just plain sex, Ellen knew she was not being shortchanged.

Jeremy was able to accomplish all that H.T. had wanted him to do and much more. They met a few people who knew Jeremy's past, and most were pleased that he had finally found a place in God's work. Others were inclined to undermine his work but, seeing that the power was on his side, they decided to go with the flow. There were others who remembered Jeremy as the banty rooster; most of them were proud of his success, because they considered him one of their own. An occasional "Hallelujah, brother" didn't phase Jeremy in the least. With the titles Dr. and College President, he was still the Holiness preacher they had always loved. The things he now advocated might not have been acceptable from someone else, but coming from Jeremy, even the most dogmatic were willing to give them consideration.

As the trip progressed, it became clear to Ellen that he was not only the choice of H.T., but also the choice of God. The days in tents with sawdust floors and two-by-four altar rails had prepared Jeremy for the job at hand. For Jeremy, it had become a crusade.

Ellen learned early in their travels that all church people were not saints. The men were not as direct as the young girl had been with Jeremy, but more than one made subtle approaches. The most blatant move was made in a church kitchen as she was helping prepare a meal for a small group having a workshop. Ellen was dicing celery; all the other women had left. Suddenly one of the men in his late forties entered the kitchen and stood very close to her. He reached around her, placed his hand on her hip, and was gradually moving it down with a gentle massaging motion. Ellen turned so he could see the knife and said, "I suggest you move your hand before I remove it permanently." He made a fast exit. Ellen never told Jeremy about this or similar things that happened. She wanted to take care of such things herself when she could. Ellen was sure if these men had known her background, they would not have taken such liberties to begin with.

Chapter IX

H.T. was amazed at the increase in enrollment when school started and immediately began to start making plans for the next summer. He even hoped his schedule would enable him to make the trip himself.

The increased enrollment made for a very hectic year and demanded full commitment on everyone's part. Ellen found herself more involved with the students than before, especially those away from home for the first time.

She tried to encourage the girls who felt they were called to preach the Gospel. These girls were allowed to teach, work with the youth, do church program planning and other jobs within the church. Many of them were very gifted, but the church would not open its doors to them as pastors. With the rigid attitude of some of the church's leaders, Ellen sometimes wondered if it would ever happen. She was frustrated.

It was Christmas break before Ellen and Jeremy could get any time away from the school. They decided to spend Christmas with Dot and Con. Just to be with Dot was a real treat for Ellen. She and Dot could spend time together, because Con seemed very much at ease with Jeremy. When Ellen commented on this, Dot said, "You have to remember, we were raised together. Jeremy will always be our little brother." Ellen was happy for them and the joy they had found in each other. Since the loss of her family, this empty feeling of being alone was always with her.

Con and Dot had moved into a new house, much larger and more elaborate. What amazed Ellen most was the suite of offices attached to the back of the house. There was not only an office for Con, but also an office for his full-time secretary, each lavishly furnished and fully equipped. Even on

Christmas day, when Con's secretary was not there, he checked his office for messages on equipment Ellen had never seen anywhere else.

Ellen asked Dot, "Does Con service all his clients from his home office now?"

"No, H.T. is Con's only client."

"What if something should happen to H.T. and Con was left without a practice?"

"We're well provided for whatever might happen."

Ellen could not imagine one person with the wealth and business to keep Con as his personal lawyer.

When they returned to school after Christmas vacation, H.T. called a meeting for January to set plans in motion for the trip in June. H.T. would be making the trip. Con and Dot would also be going. Con might leave them for a few days if an emergency should arise in the business, but hopefully this would not happen.

Ellen and Dot kept the phone lines busy the next few weeks, planning and anticipating the wonderful times they both were sure lay ahead for them. Ellen had only one regret: the loss of privacy that she and Jeremy had enjoyed on the previous trip. With that many people in such cramped quarters, things were bound to be different. Ellen didn't let this bother her for long, because just being with Dot would outweigh any inconvenience.

In late January, they met in the library of the president's residence. H.T. had a big surprise to start things off. He had leased another railcar from one of his business associates, giving them two cars! Jeremy and Ellen would have the same accommodations they had used on the last trip, the only difference being everyone would dine in their car.

The new car had two private sleeping compartments, as well as servants' quarters. H.T. and Con would be working most of every day so office facilities would occupy the rest of the space in their car. Both women would be together in Ellen's car, talking, reading, or sightseeing. There were times when Ellen and Dot were together when there would be long periods of silence. They had achieved that rare stage in their friendship where they could enjoy each other's company in complete silence.

To assist Rufus, H.T. was bringing along Bill and Ruby, a man and wife who worked for him full-time at his home. They would do the cooking and cleaning, leaving Rufus to take care of their personal needs as well as the many details of their schedule.

Con was making the trip because H.T. was ready to take the initial steps to form a more closely connected church. H.T. did not expect to make more than a beginning but he needed Con to explain the legal issues. The idea of a unified church would be hard to achieve.

Jeremy had a new agenda this trip: he must make the church members see the greater potential for service with a close-knit, unified church. All three men realized how difficult their job would be. They would face strong opposition. These were people who were used to a loosely connected church.

They started their trip in early June to a small meeting that took only one day. H.T. wanted to make sure that, if the initial presentation were not perfect, it better be before a small group and therefore not do too much damage. H.T. and Con met all day with the business committee of the convention. While not elated with their success, they did feel some progress had been made. Both men now felt that the success of the project rested in the hands of Jeremy. If he could convince the rank and file, their pressure on the leaders could swing things in their direction.

Jeremy started by talking about Christ and his twelve followers. H.T. became nervous; where was he going? They were trying to convince people to become a large unified church and Jeremy was talking about twelve followers.

Jeremy didn't keep them wondering for long. He quickly switched to the scattered twelve following the Crucifixion. As they went their separate ways, the Gospel spread rapidly, their following increased rapidly, but even this didn't accomplish the formation of a church with a world mission. Jeremy then told them the story of Paul, who traveled throughout his known world forming church bodies wherever he went. Paul did not let these churches stand alone, but kept in touch with each one through his letters and made these churches aware of the progress made in their own sister churches. He encouraged the churches to keep in touch and to support the men who were traveling, spreading the word. It was through this united effort the church was formed and became strong. Jeremy went on to say that only in this way can we become the church Christ is calling us to be. United in Christ we have the wealth, knowledge, strength, and commitment to serve. Jeremy, as usual, had inspired them to think and act. They left their first stop feeling good about what they had accomplished.

During the days, Ellen and Dot were on their own for most of the trip, except when they had to participate in social functions. Most every day the men were working, so they shopped, went to the movies, or, if the town was large enough, visited the sights of interest. Ellen had seen very little of Atlanta the year before. Dot used the week to be Ellen's tour guide. They used the opportunity to buy new clothes and also shopped for Con and Jeremy.

Ellen and Jeremy, like the year before, attended formal parties at country clubs given by business associates of H.T. On this trip, they did not spend any time at people's homes. This was the decision of H.T. because he knew that Con, being a very private person, would not feel at ease. H.T. used the excuse that they must be where they had access to the equipment available to them in their office. However, Con did receive messages every day requesting information or advice on decisions that had to be made concerning the business. These requests became so frequent that H.T. finally sent a memo to all administrative personnel not to call on Con for help unless the executive in charge felt he was not capable of making the decision without assistance. This greatly reduced the demands on Con's time; few administrators were willing to admit they were not capable of performing their duties without assistance. On this trip, it became clear to Ellen that Con was more to H.T. than legal counsel. He was the mainspring that kept his business empire moving.

They finished their work in early August and returned to the campus of Apostolic College feeling their work had been productive. Apostolic College was the name arrived at by the governing body of the church; H.T. had felt it better to let this group name the school. They did not realize how productive their work had been until they saw the large increase in enrollment. Even more encouraging was the large increase in young men planning to enter into full-time ministry. In past years these young men might have gone out untrained, but now they had witnessed the power of Dr. Jeremy Grimes and they had aspirations toward higher goals. Everyone was elated over the success of their mission and Jeremy was pleased, but not, it seemed, as exuberant as others involved. Ellen was not surprised by his reaction; she had seen the same reaction when things were going well in the past. To her, it seemed he became cautious as if he was waiting for something to happen, or feared he might do something to change everything as he had before. Ellen was sure he remembered how great things were before, when he had lost Ruth and their unborn child, and was determined not to be foolhardy again. It was part guilt, coupled with the feeling he was not worthy of such success.

On the morning of December 7, 1941, the bombs over Pearl Harbor shattered their world. Did Jeremy have a premonition of things to come? It was her first thought when the report of the Japanese bombing came over the radio. Dr. Jeremy Grimes would witness once again his world being blown apart and through no fault of his own.

Chapter X

Because of the war, there was no way the school could keep growing. By the time Jeremy and Ellen left campus to spend Christmas with Dot and Con, the student body had dropped by half. The way things were going, by spring the student body would be 75 percent female.

Their visit with Dot and Con was a part of the year Ellen looked forward to, but, try as they would, it was not the same. Con hardly had time enough to see them for meals, even though his work was done in his office at home. H.T. was converting all his manufacturing business into production of goods needed for the war. Ellen was amazed that this could be done, but even toy factories were being converted into weapons construction.

Ellen and Dot were left alone much of the time. While Con worked, Jeremy spent most of his time alone wandering around the woods and meadows that made up the surrounding countryside. Ellen was worried and expressed to Dot she didn't know what was wrong or what she might do to help him. Dot told her there wasn't anything she could do. Jeremy had been this way when Ruth died, but eventually worked through his problem. "Just be there for him."

These words came back to Ellen when they were alone. He embraced her and seemed reluctant to let her go. Though he never expressed it in words, he seemed to fear that if he released her, she would be gone forever. Ellen had no idea what was wrong. She followed the advice, "Do what you can, with what you have, where you happen to be." She simply talked to him if he wished to talk, or sat in silence if that seemed to be what he wanted. There were times when they sat for hours, her head resting on his shoulder, just listening to the sounds about them. Other times at night they had better sex than they had ever experienced. It seemed Jeremy was determined they would both experience a passion they would never forget. Ellen even became caught up in the frenzy. Looking back on those nights of lovemaking, Ellen sensed that each time was one that would never be forgotten—it would never happen again.

A few days before they were to return home, Jeremy became more like himself again. Dot assured Ellen, "This has always been Jeremy's way, once he decides how he can handle a problem."

Con and Jeremy spent more time together the last week. Ellen saw how close they were. They seemed more like brothers than friends. Dot told Ellen, whatever Jeremy's problem had been, it concerned only them, because he had not discussed it with Con. Ellen was patient because she knew if it concerned only the two of them, they should be at home when they discussed it. However, her waiting was filled with a great deal of anxiety. She knew that if Jeremy had found it so hard to come to a decision, it would definitely affect their future. But Ellen could wait because she knew now that Jeremy loved her.

Chapter XI

They returned home on January 3, 1942, the coldest night that winter. Two feet of snow covered the ground, but inside the servants had a roaring fire waiting for them in the den fireplace. The cook served them mugs of hot chocolate. Ellen let the servants retire for the evening.

She and Jeremy curled up in front of the fire. It wasn't long before they were warm, but Ellen had a cold, dark feeling that would not go away. It was the same cold that had gripped her deep inside when she heard her father read Little Skip's letter so many years before. He had told her father he must find a way to get Bruce released from prison before it was too late. Having those feelings was not only painful, but also fearful.

Jeremy had been struggling with what to tell her, but once he started, the words rushed out. He seemed powerless to stop them.

"Ellen, this is the hardest decision I've ever faced. I have come to love you more than anyone or anything except God. I would find it impossible to face it if I were not sure it is God's will and his task for me—I have no choice. I have received God's call to join the service as a chaplain. If it were not that I must leave you, it would be easy, but the thought of being without you for even a short time tears at my soul."

Ellen was stunned. She felt as if her heart were being ripped from her body. Ellen had realized that she had come to love Jeremy, but how deep that love had become was overpowering.

She quickly recovered. "It won't be forever. I will wait as long as it takes for you to answer God's call."

She still had the feeling that another chapter of her life was coming to an end.

H.T. had to be told, so the next morning Jeremy invited him to come over for lunch. When Jeremy told H.T. what he felt called to do, he was surprised to find that H.T. was one step ahead. He had been conferring with friends in government about a training program for men who would be entering the service as chaplains. The chaplains' branch of service was not adequate to serve the vast influx of civilians who would be entering the military in the next year. The training program was necessary to familiarize them with the many problems they would face that they had not encountered in civilian churches. His friends had agreed with him that their school was the ideal spot for such a program, and Jeremy would be an asset as its instructor. H.T. added that Jeremy could head the program as a civilian or as a member of the armed forces. Because the new chaplains would be entering service as commissioned officers, Jeremy felt it would be better if he were also a member of the service. Everyone was in agreement, and Jeremy became a captain in the Chaplains Corps.

Chapter XII

Before taking over his new responsibilities, Jeremy had to leave for a six-week course in the duties of a chaplain under combat conditions. This seemed like a short course for such an important undertaking, but people everywhere were taking on important and dangerous tasks with very limited training. In the more dangerous jobs, it caused casualties, but there was no other way to become a nation at war in such a short time.

Jeremy was gone. The nights in the president's house were lonely for Ellen. Her only break in the boredom was when school business or social functions demanded her time. H.T. had assumed this part of Jeremy's duties. The dean took over the everyday administrative work. H.T. had let it be known that as long as Jeremy was busy with the war, Ellen would remain a resident in the president's quarters.

Jeremy had very little difficulty absorbing the regimented military way of doing things. At the same time, he witnessed the difficult time many of the older ministers had adjusting to new ways.

Jeremy met with his first class of fifty and proceeded to give them mountains of work and long hours of sorting through facts and figures. The older pastors hadn't been used to such work at breakneck speed. Jeremy let them know that millions of young men were enduring training that was even more rigorous than what they were experiencing. These soldiers were going to face situations where they would need all the faith, assurance, and guidance they could give them.

The greatest thorn in Jeremy's side was the pastors who insisted on sticking to prescribed church dogma. One afternoon things reached the boiling point when the Sacrament of the Lord's Supper was discussed. Several followed the doctrine of "closed communion." Some, thinking it sounded better, preferred to call it "close communion." Jeremy told them, regardless of what name they chose to use, it was one Christian refusing to come to the Lord's Table with another Christian. He reminded them what Jesus said, "Do this in remembrance of me."

There was one minister who insisted his church doctrine would not allow him to serve communion to just anyone, even if they did profess to be followers of Christ.

"Suppose your group was getting ready to go into combat and it was certain that some of the men would not survive. Search your heart—knowing these men might never live to see another day, could you refuse to serve them at the Lord's Table?"

The man would not be moved, "My denomination does not allow it."

"You are fortunate you serve a God capable of divine love and forgiveness, because if I were God, I would present you with a one-way ticket to hell." Jeremy walked out in anger.

Ellen could still see the anger in his face when he returned home. He went directly to his study. She became worried when he did not come out after three hours, and she called Dot. Dot laughed and assured her there wasn't anything to worry about. Something has happened to upset him and "what Con and I call his righteous indignation has boiled to the surface." Dot assured her Jeremy would work through it in a few hours, and everything would be normal again. Dot was right—four hours later, Jeremy emerged from his study as if nothing had happened.

The matter of church doctrine became taboo in the class and everything went smoothly for the remainder of the course. Jeremy was not fully convinced they were ready, but prayed their faith in God would see them through.

Chapter XIII

It would be two weeks before the next class would be ready to start. Jeremy requested duty with a group on maneuvers at Ft. Oglethorpe, Georgia. He wanted to witness firsthand what his students would be facing once they were on duty.

When he returned home, he expressed to Ellen his concern that many of the men he was training were not capable of filling the needs of the ones they must serve. "But they are men who have established beliefs, and they will be able to strengthen each other. They face the possibility of death every day, even in training."

Jeremy settled in with his new class and found them much more dedicated than the first group. Many were fresh out of divinity school, and the rigorous schedule was something they had become used to. Church doctrine was avoided by both Jeremy and the students. Jeremy wondered if his reputation had made its way through the grapevine. Everything went smoothly, and Jeremy spent more time on physically conditioning the men than he had with the previous group.

He had seen the importance of getting the men in physical condition for the rigorous life some of them would face. Jeremy suggested that, whenever possible, every new chaplain spend some time on maneuvers. He had seen enough to know that most of the first graduates from his classes would never receive any additional training. At this early stage of the war, every branch needed men so badly that training was kept to a minimum. Jeremy knew that time and need would dictate every decision.

Jeremy received orders to report to Ft. Oglethorpe for maneuvers and also was promoted to major. He returned home one week before the new class was to begin. Ellen knew immediately he was trying to work through a new problem. There was no doubt in her mind another decision was going to be made that would affect their future. Jeremy didn't keep her wondering for long but was eager to discuss with her what was bothering him.

There was a catch in Jeremy's voice as he told Ellen, "This group—they are not men—they are boys! We have been at war for a year now, and some of them are in their early twenties. Many are fresh out of high school. These boys are not old enough to have faith that will sustain them through the hell of war. These boys need me. It is my duty to apply for transfer to a unit going into combat."

They didn't sleep much that night but held each other, trying to comfort themselves and each other. Early the next morning, Jeremy called H.T. and invited him over for breakfast. After they had eaten, they went into Jeremy's study.

Ellen knew that H.T. had come to admire and respect Jeremy, but his reaction was more like a father called on to sign papers that could cost his son's life. "With your rank of major, they will want to assign you to one of the larger bases, not to a combat unit."

Jeremy could not be swayed. H.T., against his own wishes, used his influence to get Jeremy reassigned. After Jeremy finished with the class, ready to start, they would get a two-week vacation and then Jeremy would join a combat unit and immediately embark for Europe.

Ellen and Jeremy had many last-minute arrangements to make preparing for their vacation and for the time they would be separated. H.T. informed them that the urgent need for chaplains had been met. There would be no more classes at the school once the present class graduated. Otherwise, things remained the same. Ellen would continue to live on campus in the president's house and assist H.T. and the dean in running the school until Jeremy returned. They were hard-pressed to get all their affairs in order and still plan for their two-week vacation.

Jeremy knew how much Ellen loved Florida and made plans to spend their first week there. After their week in Florida, they would go to the hills of East Tennessee where Jeremy spent his childhood. Ellen realized that Jeremy wanted to see his home one more time and he especially wanted her to see it with him. Ellen was also eager to see the mountains and know the kind of place that produced outstanding people like Dot, Con, and Jeremy. She especially wanted to talk with Polly, the head of the orphanage. She hoped to find out about Jeremy's past, and how he came to be there. Dot had only told Ellen sketches of their past life, and she wanted to learn all she could. Ellen had heard that the mountain people were very private people, but she hoped once Polly saw how much she loved Jeremy, she would be willing to shed some light on Jeremy's past.

Chapter XIV

Ellen had fond memories of every trip she had taken to Florida, but this time was special. H.T. made his private railcar available to them.

The sound of train wheels and whistles still turned her on, but now in a different way. This time, Ellen, for the first time, found the special joy that comes with sex motivated by love. She had not realized that her admiration and respect for Jeremy had become a deep love that controlled her every thought and act.

They spent much of their time in Florida walking on the beaches that were not under control of the military. All around them were preparations for war and a frantic effort to make sure the enemy didn't surprise the United States again. All this constant activity around them made it impossible for them to shut out the world and think only of the time they had left to spend together.

The beaches were closed at night and were patrolled by soldiers with dogs. There were also towers where spotters watched for enemy aircraft day and night. Beaches that had once been a haven for lovers now seemed hostile. They desperately wanted to forget the conflict that permeated all of life around them, but it was hard to do, because even the absence of light during the nightly blackouts was a grim reminder.

After a week of these constant reminders of a nation at war, they were happy to leave Florida and head for the solitude of the mountains. Ellen was not unfamiliar with the mountains, but she had never seen the isolation, poverty, and lack of opportunity she now witnessed in the area where Jeremy grew up. Electric lights, indoor plumbing, and running water were things these people had never seen. Ellen would always wonder how a girl and two boys could come from such surroundings and achieve what Dot, Con, and Jeremy had. It was the most stunning example of grit, courage, and determination. It made her rise from bootlegger's daughter to wife of a college president seem insignificant.

Here in the mountains they found solitude and fairly comfortable living quarters. At the orphanage where Jeremy was fondly remembered, they were able to rent a log cabin from a staff member who had been called into service. The cabin was not what they were used to, but nice. They took their meals with the staff and children in the orphanage dining room. The food was nourishing and satisfying. They had not come to the mountains looking for luxury but to enjoy peace and quiet and to be alone. They were trying to escape for a short time a world they knew would soon take complete control of their lives.

Jeremy showed her the places he had loved as a youth and they hiked the trails to remote places of beauty. Ellen was most moved when Jeremy showed her the places he had come to pray as he struggled with the driving force that would control his future.

When the sun was warm in the early afternoon, they often sat for hours in silence, the only noise coming from birds or animals. At these times, Ellen was sure Jeremy was once again seeking strength from the eternal source of power that he might be prepared for the task that lay ahead.

One afternoon sitting by a clear mountain stream, listening as it cascaded over the rocks and down the mountain, she looked into Jeremy's face. What she saw brought a chill to her heart. She realized for the first time he not only wanted her to see this place he loved, he was driven by a desire to come home once more where his life had begun, knowing he might never come home again. Ellen thought of the millions of young men and boys who must be experiencing the same feelings in many parts of the world. A chill caused her to tremble. Jeremy, thinking she might be getting cold, suggested they return to the cabin.

There they rested for the remainder of the afternoon, cuddled in a warm feather bed covered by beautiful quilts created by the skilled hands of the mountain women. Their lovemaking was no less passionate, but Ellen felt a tenderness between them that made it more satisfying and complete.

Chapter XV

That evening, after they had finished their meal in the orphanage dining room, Miss Polly asked them to visit with her in her quarters. Polly's bedroom was the same as those of the other staff members, but she had taken an additional bedroom and made it into a combination office and parlor. Miss Polly carried an oil lamp into the parlor and placed it into a wall bracket. The faint lamp light always gave Ellen an eerie feeling. She could understand why the mailman considered the place to be haunted, or as he had said, "hanted."

Miss Polly came right to the point, asking Jeremy what he had in mind about visiting Aunt Mag. Jeremy said he was waiting for the best possible weather and was trying to decide if he should take Ellen with him. Miss Polly advised against such a difficult trip, especially this time of year when a sudden change in the weather could make it necessary to stay overnight. Jeremy told Ellen that Aunt Mag lived in the next cove just across the mountain behind them; it was a good two-hour hike. Ellen agreed that it seemed more than she should attempt, not being an experienced hiker.

Miss Polly asked Ellen to spend the day with her so they could get to know each other better. This was what Ellen had hoped; she wanted to know more about Dot, Con, and Jeremy, and their life at the orphanage.

The next morning, the weather was bright and clear. Jeremy was ready to leave after an early breakfast. Ellen asked him not to come back if the weather turned bad, so Jeremy promised to stay over if there was any change.

The weather was cool, but there was a warm sunshine, so Ellen and Miss Polly put on warm wraps and sat in rockers on the front porch enjoying the morning sun. Ellen had heard that the mountain people were very suspicious and inclined to be very reluctant to answer questions if a person became too inquisitive. She was eager to know all she could about Jeremy, but was afraid Polly would clam up if she were too direct. Ellen started by remarking that the mailman who brought them up the mountain had told Jeremy the barn was still "hanted." She was familiar with the word "hanted" but did not understand why the mailman had called the orphanage building a barn and why he would think it was haunted.

"There is a story back of that," said Polly, "and we have plenty of time so I will tell you all of it."

Miss Polly stood and asked Ellen to follow her. "The architecture of this building is really just a cantilever barn. If you look closely at most of the barns in the mountains you will see the resemblance. Imagine it without the front porch. Then, where the door is, replace it with a door wide enough to accommodate a team pulling a wagon load of hay."

They went inside. Ellen looked around the great room. On both sides were the bedrooms.

"Imagine the bedrooms as stalls. Over these stalls, on each side of the great room, were haylofts, which are now balconies where the children sleep."

Steps on each side of the great room led up to the balconies. Standing in the great room, they looked at a fireplace, so large it served as the dividing wall.

"If you were actually standing in a cantilever barn, the fireplace wall would not be there, and you would be looking at another barn door on the back."

In back of the fireplace wall were the dining room and kitchen. "Before this lodge was built, all I had was a cabin only large enough to keep six small children. How we finally got this building, making it possible to become an orphanage and school, is another story. It is a story that involves some strange new characters who are still a part of mountain storytelling.

"Old Ike Morgan lived about four miles on up the mountain. He was not really old, but mean and ornery.

"Old Ike had a redheaded wife, Big M, and the men said she was built like a brick 'shit house.' I doubt any one of them had ever seen a brick outhouse. Be that as it may, Old Ike didn't give a tinker's damn about anything or anybody except Big M.

"I was never around them but the story was her name was really Ema, but Big Ike never called her anything except Big M. I have always said, no matter how mean a person might be, there is always something that person loves, and Old Ike dearly loved that redheaded woman.

"They kept to themselves, and Old Ike made moonshine whiskey and built cantilever barns. The only help Ike had was a young Indian boy from the reservation over in North Carolina. Ike always called him Little Chief, and rumor had it, Ike was so mean, only an Indian would work for him.

"I seldom heard anything about Ike and his woman, but somehow word did reach me that Big M was pregnant. Whoever it was told me said they hadn't contacted the midwife because Big M said she was as strong as any heifer and could drop her own calf.

"I didn't give it any more thought, because at the time I had six small children and only one helper, so it was impossible for me to visit anyone.

"It was really early one snowy winter morning when there was a loud knock at the door. It was that young Indian carrying a baby wrapped in a feed sack, and they were both nearly frozen. I let him inside and, after cleaning the baby and giving it some sugar water, sat down with Little Chief. When I asked Little Chief what had happened, it was quite apparent he had helped with the birthing. He said he had seen more than one Indian woman give birth, but he had never seen anything like this. He said labor had gone on all day and most of the night before the baby was finally born. From the way he told it, I figure the baby came feet first and he and Old Ike didn't know what to do. The baby was finally born alive, but Big M didn't survive. If they had had the experience of a midwife, things might have been different, but then again, maybe not. It isn't unusual for women to die in childbirth here in the mountains.

"Little Chief said Old Ike was completely out of his mind, and he had left with the baby because he was afraid Old Ike might kill all three of them. At daybreak, Little Chief said he should go back and help Old Ike bury Big M, but he would come back as soon as Old Ike regained his senses.

"It was one whole month before I saw hide or hair of either one of them. Then one morning, Little Chief and Old Ike came strolling in as if nothing had happened. Ike said, 'I want to see M's baby.' He had never called her anything but M or Big M, so I guess he didn't mean to change now that she was dead. Him saying M's baby and not our baby really concerned me because that baby looked like an Indian.

"I didn't know what to expect, but it was just as if he didn't notice one thing. He just said, 'So that's Little M.' He didn't even touch the little baby girl, just stood and looked. After a brief interval, he turned and walked outside.

"I told Ike we were crowded and I didn't have room for another baby and needed to know what he planned to do with his little girl.

'I can no longer stay in the mountains, but I don't want you to bear a burden that's not yours.'

"Then Ike made me a proposition. If I would keep the child, he would build me facilities large enough to keep forty children and six staff people. Ike said the only thing he knew how to build was a cantilever barn, but he could put a foundation under it and anybody could build a floor. He outlined for me how he would close in the stalls and make bedrooms. For heat, he could build a large fireplace at the end of the great room. He said with steps to the loft, we could sleep twenty boys on one side and twenty girls on the other side. I told Ike it all sounded great, but we still had to cook and would need a dining room. It was then that Ike came up with the idea of a kitchen and dining room under a shed-type roof built behind the fireplace wall. I liked the idea and decided to press my luck by suggesting a front porch covered by a shed roof.

"For reasons that only Ike knows, he decided to be agreeable and it was decided that he and Little Chief would start getting supplies together and be ready to begin with the first spring thaw. We had an early spring that year, and they were able to have everything under roof by fall.

"During those eight months he didn't pay much attention to Little M, but at times, when he didn't know I was watching, I could see him looking her over. It bothered me because every month that passed, that black hair got longer and she looked more like an Indian. I was relieved when the time came that they were nearly finished. Then the day came when the only thing left to do was to top off the chimney. If you don't know what that means, step out into the yard and you can see a large flat rock covering the top of the chimney supported by six rocks spaced around the outer edge of the chimney. This allows the smoke to escape out the top of the chimney without allowing the rain to come in. This was a big event, because it meant everything was finished, so we all gathered outside to watch.

"Ike was on the roof and the rock was cradled in a burlap sack with Little Chief on the ground lifting it up with a rope and pulley. I was watching closely as Ike braced himself against the chimney and reached out to maneuver the rock into place. When Ike touched the rock, it seemed to just leap out of that burlap pouch, and Little Chief never knew what hit him. He was killed instantly. We buried him the next day under that large oak just across the clearing.

"Right to this very day, I am convinced I witnessed a murder, but there is not one thing I could testify to that would have any merit. Old Ike managed to get that flat rock mounted on the chimney without any help the day after we buried Little Chief. He left the mountains that night and hasn't been seen or heard from since.

"Little M grew into a beautiful young woman and left the mountains when she was twenty. She still had those Indian features, but the men swore the body was a dead ringer for Big M. Little M married well and is one of our students who didn't forget where she started. She, along with many other past students, sends money regularly. We don't have any large endowments, but also we no longer want for money.

"Little Chief is still with us and always will be, because he has become part of the mountain folklore. When the mountain people sit around the fire on cold winter nights, they tell stories about Little Chief. As those stories are told and retold, they become bigger and Little Chief becomes greater. The mountain people call him Little Chief Panther, and after we fix us a cup of tea, I will tell you that story and why the mailman said the place is 'hanted.'"

Chapter XVI

"After Little Chief was buried and Old Ike disappeared, things gradually settled down. I started to say 'returned to normal,' but that was not the case. We quickly started to fill the new building and our six babies grew to twenty. There was a steady flow of orphans and most of the children were small and could not help with the work, and for a while it was a real burden. When I put out a call for help, I was astonished at the number of women from the large churches who volunteered to become a part of our staff. Some of the women needed a place to stay but many others were looking for a worthwhile cause to serve.

"After we brought our staff up to six, things did start to stabilize and our growth stabilized. We were able to plan our agenda for the future and start looking for qualified teachers.

"We had been in the house about a year when things out of the ordinary began to happen. The teachers reported to me that some students had been going back to bed during the day because they could see where their heads had rested on the pillow. It was not always the same student and everyone denied it, so I just let things slide. Then lamps would be found burning and the person who used it last would swear the lamp was out when they left it. There was already talk around the area that Little Chief was haunting the place, so I thought some of the older children were just playing jokes. Then again, you must remember the people of these mountains are mostly of Scottish descent, and they are great believers in the supernatural.

"The thing that really got my attention happened when Little M was just a little over one year old. She became ill and was running a very high fever. I was sitting with her through the night and bathing her face with cold compresses. I kept hearing pacing outside my door, up and down the great room. I thought it was probably one of the teachers who was worried and couldn't sleep. I decided one of us should get some rest and opened my door to tell her to relieve me for a few hours. The pacing stopped immediately and there was no one there. I went back to my chair by Little M's bed and the pacing started again, just like before, up and down the length of the great room. I opened the door again, but just as before, the pacing stopped and there was no one there. The pacing kept up all night, but I never opened the door again.

"The next morning M was a little better, so while one of the other women sat with her I decided to get some sleep. I had been in bed only about an hour when they awakened me and said there was an old woman at the door who insisted she must see me immediately.

"When I went to the door, there stood an old woman I had never met. She could have been in her sixties, but when I looked into her eyes, I had the feeling I was looking back into eternity. I can't say what caused the feeling except her eyes seemed to reveal all things and at the same time revealed nothing at all. She said, 'My name is Mag. Where is the girl?' That was how I met Mag. I had heard about Mag and I knew where she lived, and riding her old mule named Blue, she left home long before daylight to arrive here that early. I didn't ask how she knew M was sick, but simply asked why did you start before daylight, it wasn't that urgent. Her reply was, 'I couldn't sleep anyway, and Little Chief wouldn't let me alone.'

"Mag brought in a variety of plants, berries, and roots. There were some I recognized, but not very many. Mag stood by M's bed and looked her over from head to toe. Then she stared into her eyes for a long time. Mag then went into the kitchen and asked that we get her a small kettle filled with water. Placing the kettle on the stove, Mag started filling a small bag with herbs that she selected from her stock. When the water reached a rolling boil, Mag removed it from the stove and dropped the bag into the water much as you would if you were making tea. This produced a very dark and strong smelling liquid that she gave M every hour for the next six hours. At the end of six hours, Little M looked much better, her temperature had dropped and she was well on her way to recovery. Mag loaded her items, said she will be fine now, but if anything goes wrong, I will know and I will come back.

"This was the last we heard from Mag for a long time except for tales some of the mountain people told and a lot of these were so wild we chose to ignore them. Also, Little Chief was quiet and everything was normal.

"I started out to tell you how he came to be called not just that Indian or Little Chief, but Little Chief Panther. Of course, most of the mountain people shorten Panther to Panter.

"There were panthers in the mountains in those days and usually they stayed away from people unless their food supply was scarce. Even then they usually attacked livestock and stayed away from people. It happened on a bright summer morning when M was two years old.

"We were having a staff meeting in the great room and the children were all playing here in the front yard. Suddenly, one of the older boys said, 'Quick, Miss Polly,' and the fear in his voice brought me to the front door in a hurry. Little M was about thirty yards from the tree line and creeping toward her was the only panther I ever saw close up. It may have been because I was so frightened, but to this day I am sure that panther was at least ten feet long from its head to its tail. I froze in my tracks, but as calmly as I could, told Little M not to move a muscle. That panther was easing toward her, its belly close to the ground, and I knew if she moved it would spring. One of the other women was standing right behind me loading the high-powered rifle we used to hunt deer. Without me even turning around, she placed the rifle in my hand and I raised it to my shoulder ready to shoot. Before I could pull the trigger, there he was—Little Chief was standing between Little M and that panther. The Little Chief just stood there not moving a muscle, but that panther backed off visibly shaken and went slinking back into the woods. As the panther disappeared, I looked back toward Little M and Little Chief, but Little Chief was no longer there. So, today when the mountain people tell their stories, it is Little Chief Panther and how all the panthers fear him.

"That was the last panther I ever saw, but for years we could still hear them at night farther back in the mountains. They scream like a woman in great pain and then when the mountain people hear a panther they always say Little Chief Panther has them on the move tonight. The hunters say they still hear them scream farther back in the mountains, but not close by. The women in this area tell their children they don't need to fear the panther anymore because Little Chief Panther doesn't allow them in this part of the mountains.

"There are those who say the Little Chief still roams these mountains and haunts this building, but it isn't true. Little Chief Panther was Little M's guardian angel and when she left the mountains, his work there was done.

"People often ask me, 'Polly, do you really believe in this spirit world you are telling about?' I can only say my parents came to these mountains straight from Scotland and they brought with them strong beliefs about the supernatural, but, personally, I have always been too busy with the things of this world to think much about another. There is one thing for certain: I can't deny the things I saw with my own eyes."

Ellen had never heard such strange stories and didn't know what to think, but she certainly would not dare challenge anything Polly had told her. Ellen made a mental note to ask Jeremy.

Ellen had determined not to ask questions for fear Polly would stop talking. But in spite of her resolve, found herself asking, "Who is this woman Mag? Is she really Jeremy's aunt?"

"No," replied Polly, "as far as we know, she is not related to Jeremy. But the fact of the matter is we know nothing at all about Jeremy, where Jeremy came from, his family or his background. There isn't one clue.

"I wanted to tell you about Dot and Con first because they came to me first and, as you know, are about three years older than Jeremy. To tell you about Mag, it is necessary to tell you about Jeremy, because he brought her into our lives. Who is she? Some would say spiritualist, others psychic or clairvoyant. Then there are others who would say fortune-teller and still others who would call her that old witch, but not loud enough for her to hear.

"Our involvement with Mag started on a cold night in December, in fact, about one week before Christmas. The weather was bitter cold, the snow three feet deep and still coming down. About one o'clock in the morning there was a knock at the door. Thinking someone might be in trouble, I rushed to answer it. I opened the door, but no one was there. As I started to close the door, I realized there was something on the porch. Moving closer, I saw it was a cradle, and instantly looked around to see if anyone was near. When I looked toward the woods where the panther came from that day, I saw movement, but could not tell if it was man or beast. There is only one thing I am sure of—whoever left him was waiting there to make sure he was taken in. He was not a newborn, but could not have been more than a week old. The cradle was like hundreds of others made by expectant fathers throughout these mountains. There were no clues that would indicate where he came from or who he belonged to, and never would be.

"It is now that Mag becomes a part of this tale. We have no idea what part she played in Jeremy's coming to us, or what part she still plays, only that she made herself a part of Jeremy's life and a part of everyone's life who was close to him.

"It was about six the following morning when old Mag rode in. She was riding a mule she called Old Blue and that mule was as near dead as a mule could get and still be on its feet. Old Mag looked like death warmed over and was nearly frozen stiff. That trip through the cold and snow had taken her at least five hours and would have killed most people. We punched up the fire in the big fireplace and she stood there for nearly fifteen minutes not saying one word. The hot fire melted the snow and ice off her bearskin coat and the water collected at her feet. The first words she spoke were, 'Where is the boy?' I asked what boy? The anger flared in Mag's eyes like coals of fire. She answered, 'Don't play with me, Polly, you know what boy.' I can be quite bullheaded if I am so inclined so I asked what do you know about the boy, Mag? She instantly became very calm and replied, 'You really don't want to know, Polly.' Turning, we both walked into the bedroom where he lay in the cradle. She looked at that tiny baby boy with love and joy, feelings it was difficult for me to associate with old Mag. She stood there a very long time with the look of a person standing before a shrine. The feeling came over me—this is an event this woman has waited for all her life. I could not explain it, but the emotion she was feeling seemed unreal.

"Mag stayed with us until about noon and I tried to get her not to make that trip again until the weather got better, but she was determined to leave at once. Standing on the porch, she turned to me and said, 'Polly, you have been blessed. God has chosen you to care for one of his special people.'

"Mag still didn't come around on a regular schedule, but we knew if Jeremy became the least bit under the weather, old Mag would come riding across the mountain. Quite often some mountain man would drop by bringing something we could use and saying I owed Mag and she said to bring it to the school. People we had never met started coming by with fresh killed bear or deer and at Thanksgiving we could always expect at least three turkeys. These people apparently went to Mag needing help with their lives and she used what they owed her to help the school.

"There is more to tell you about Jeremy, but you will learn most of it as I tell about Dot. They were close from the beginning and it was Dot who gave him the name Jeremy. Dot is the only child born to one of our girls and then raised here. Her mother's name was Lottie. Lottie lived with her mother and father just at the foot of the mountain and they made a modest living farming. Her Father died and Lottie and her mother stayed on the farm but just kept a small garden and canned enough for the two of them. During the winter the two of them made quilts and sold them to the merchants who came into the mountains buying things for their shops in Gatlinburg.

"The school at this time was growing very fast and we badly needed quilts. I contacted Lottie's mother, whose name was Edna, and asked her if she could make us some quilts. We couldn't afford the kind of quilts she made for resale, but just something warm and serviceable. Edna said she could do that, but when we were alone told me she didn't want pay, but just a promise from me. She said she was suffering from the same consumption that had taken her husband, and when she died, Lottie would be alone. Lottie was already fifteen, but I agreed as long as she needed a place she could live with us. For the next two years they kept us supplied with quilts. Edna died when Lottie was seventeen and she came to live with us. Lottie was well educated for a mountain girl because her mother was educated and felt it necessary to give her daughter all the education she was capable of giving. The idea that girls do not need to be educated is the biggest obstacle we have had to fight here in the mountains. But I am wandering away from my story. To tell you how beautiful Lottie was is easy because Dot looks just like her mother. Dot also has her mother's personality and love of life. Dot never knew her mother because Lottie died when Dot was born, but I am getting ahead of my story. That's the trouble with getting old; you remember so much you get it all mixed up in the telling.

"Lottie was nineteen when a logging company came into the mountains to cut timber. There was a young man in charge of the company who couldn't have been more than twenty-one years old. He was in charge because his family owned the company, but it was not like what you would expect—he was quite capable and dedicated to his work. He was respected by his men, in spite of his age, and he worked just like he expected everyone else to do. When he and Lottie met, it seemed they were meant for each other. Mike and Lottie courted for a full year and I was very strict with Lottie, but he never complained, and he did everything according to my rules. They were married after the first year and started housekeeping in a small log cabin that Lottie's folks had left her. There was only one thing that bothered me—none of his family came to the wedding, and Mike and Lottie never went to visit them. I felt I had a special obligation to Lottie so one day I just asked him point-blank what was going on. Mike didn't hedge one bit, but told me they would always live in the mountains because he knew his Mother and knew she would never approve of Lottie. He said, 'My life is here now and it is here we will stay.' I felt like he should have enough backbone to stand up to his mother and him saying he did not wish to have Lottie subjected to his mother was just a way out for him. As usual, when we judge without knowing the facts, we are wrong, but that seems to be a widespread human weakness. He was good to Lottie and they had been married a little over a year when Lottie came to tell me she was pregnant. They were both delighted and spent all their spare time making things they would need and also building on to the cabin to make room for a nursery. Mike was worried, as most men are, and wanted Lottie to let him take her to a large city so she could be cared for in a hospital by a doctor. Lottie was amused and told him women had been having babies delivered by the midwife for years and there wasn't one thing for him to worry about. I was there with the midwife when Dot was born and to me it seemed like a normal delivery. I have always felt from the way Lottie died, she had a bad heart and none of us knew it.

"I took Dot home with me that night and some of Mike's workmen stayed with him. We buried Lottie the next day and he wandered around like a zombie. It was evident to everyone that Mike was completely out of touch with everything going on around him. I knew he was not capable of taking care of Dot, so we kept her here at the school and didn't hear anything from Mike for two weeks. He wandered in here one morning looking like a man whose world had caved in on him. Mike said, 'As much as I loved these mountains, I can no longer stand the sight of them. The place where Lottie and I met and the places we enjoyed so much together now make me physically ill. I was fully committed to spend the rest of my life here with Lottie but without her it is impossible to spend another day.' Mike went on to say if I would keep Dot here with me he would send money every month and the money would be sufficient to eliminate all financial strain. I tried to tell him he should take Dot home with him and let her live with the people who were her family, but again, he simply said he could not subject her to the treatment she would receive from his mother. I told Mike I would be happy to let Dot live with us, and though I did not say it to him, I felt again he was shirking his duty.

"Mike left the mountains that day and never returned, but true to his word, money arrived each month and it was a sizable amount. I used the money when I needed it, but most of it was saved for Dot's education. There is something else about that money shared only by Dot and myself. I am going to tell you, Ellen, because as Jeremy's wife, you should know. The financing for Dot, Con, and Jeremy's education came from that money. Dot insisted it was the way things must be and only the two of us should know."

Ellen could not resist asking, "Why did you feel it was necessary to tell me this secret?" She was surprised when Polly replied, "Because you have joined Mag, Dot, and me as the power and driving force behind two very powerful men."

Polly, after answering Ellen's question, paused for such a long time, Ellen thought she was going to stop talking, but she finally picked up her story where she had left off. "The money came for five years, and then suddenly it stopped. I didn't hear anything for several months, and one day a logger who had worked for Mike came by without any preliminary statement. He just blurted out, 'I thought you might need to know the girl's father died.' I thanked him but left it at that. I felt if Mike didn't want his family to know about Dot when he was living, they didn't need to know now. A few weeks later I was sitting here on the porch, soaking up the sun, when a horse-drawn carriage pulled into the clearing. A woman got out and headed for the porch, and my first thought was that has to be the ugliest face I have ever seen on a woman. It was not a face that was really unattractive, but was ugly because of the plain cussedness it reflected. She didn't introduce herself, ask who are you, say go to hell, kiss my ass, or pass the time of day in any manner. She said right out, 'I want to see the bastard that slut Lottie claimed is my granddaughter.' As a general rule, I am slow to anger, but she brought my blood to a boil real fast. I said, 'Old woman, you can see Dot, but if you make one more nasty remark about her or her dear departed mother, I will personally whip your ass all the way to the foot of the mountain.' I think she knew I would because she took a seat on the porch and remained quiet while I went for Dot. I brought Dot out on the porch and told her the lady wished to visit and talk with her, but I remained on the porch where I could hear what was said. They didn't say very much to each other. She just asked the questions most people would ask a young child. Dot was very polite, but her relief was evident when the visit was over. Dot went back into the house and I walked her to her carriage so she could say whatever she wished to say without Dot hearing. She said, 'I have no interest in her and there will be no money coming from me.' I said I appreciate that very much, then turned and walked away. I don't know if she thought she might find a girl as ugly and wretched as herself or one she might train to be as big a bitch, but whatever she came looking for, she didn't find and we never heard from her again. Dot never mentioned her and I am sure never realized who she was, and I will never tell her.

"That night I asked God to forgive me for passing judgment on Dot's father and I thanked God and asked him to thank Mike for keeping that mean-spirited bitch out of Dot's life."

Chapter XVII

Polly sat silent for quite a while and Ellen wondered if she was gathering her thoughts or just resting before starting her story again. Whatever the reason, once she started talking again, there was never a pause, just a constant flow of words.

"The way Con came to us was not quite as dramatic as the arrival of Dot and Jeremy, but there has never been anything you might call dramatic about Con. The first time I saw Con, he was only three and he was just as shy, just as focused, determined, and dedicated as he is today. It is hard for most people to understand Con, but those of us who knew his parents fully understand him.

"The three of them came riding in here one day with the mailman. I had sent out an urgent call to the churches for help because we had suddenly acquired more children than our staff could care for. A man and wife team would have been wonderful in most cases, but this couple, I realized right off, was not the answer to our prayers. Because most of our children were small at that time, it was necessary for our staff to do a lot of hard labor. In the summer, we had our own garden and pastured as many cows as needed. We also cut our wood for the big fireplace and the cook stove. It would take all summer to cut enough wood to last through the winter. Carrying enough wood to last through a cold winter day was a back-breaking job. All the women on staff at that time were hardened to this kind of work, but I knew this couple could not stand it. As badly as I needed help, I tried to persuade them not to stay, but they would not be denied. They were certain God had called them to serve the people of the mountains and they could not refuse his call. I was not persuaded, but I learned long ago not to stand

64

between people and what they considered God's will for their lives, so I gave in and let them stay. She was an excellent teacher and he was an outstanding financial manager. Ten years later they would have been an ideal addition to our staff, but they were in the wrong place at the wrong time. They were not physically strong people, and looking at them, it was obvious they had never done manual labor.

"Con's parents were good people and they tried to carry their share of the load, but they were just not physically able to stand the rigors of mountain living. At that time, even more than today, it was hard for people to survive in the mountains, if they were not born here. They both died the second winter, and Con became one of our family.

"It seems that I talk a lot about death, but we do run an orphanage and that keeps us closer to death than most people.

"Con, Dot, and Jeremy were our youngest, and I suppose it was only natural that they became very close from the first, or it could be it was just one of those things that was meant to be.

"Con and Dot were only two or three years older than Jeremy, but they cared for him from the very beginning. When Jeremy was two, like all two-year-olds, he demanded constant attention. This was never a problem because the staff knew that, like two shadows, Con and Dot were always nearby.

"From the beginning, it was apparent to all the staff that these three were the most outstanding children we had ever cared for. All three excelled in every way, and each one had their own unique talents.

"Dot's grandmother had been familiar with herbs and had kept a ledger listing the illnesses each could be used for. Lottie had kept it, so as soon as Dot could read, I let her study it. I learned long ago that special talents are often passed down through families and it didn't take long to see that Dot had received her grandmother's mind for healing. Dot became our live-in nurse when she was only ten. You can't realize the importance of these women who could heal.

"The majority of the people born here in the mountains live their entire lives and never see a doctor. Old Mag came to visit about the time Dot had started caring for the sick and, as usual, she came for a purpose. Mag brought a large supply of her herbs and showed Dot how they were used. Mag never disputed anything Dot's grandmother said concerning the herbs, but simply showed Dot how to prepare each one. Mag also added other uses for several of the herbs, giving Dot the benefit of her knowledge as well as her grandmother's.

"Mag spent the night with us and the following day took Dot into the mountains to show her where each herb could be found."

Ellen could not help asking Polly how it was Mag always showed up at a time when she was needed and always knew the reason for her visit. Polly said she was way past trying to understand how Mag knew when she was needed and what she was needed for, but just came to accept it was a natural happening.

"The three children started making trips into the mountains to obtain the herbs Dot needed, and word spread about her ability to heal. It became quite common for people to drop by to tell Dot about their ailments and to seek help from her when she was only twelve.

By the time Dot was thirteen, people started coming by at night asking Dot to come visit a loved one who was too ill to leave their bed. Dot never refused, and Con and Jeremy always went with her. I still worried about them because like every place, we have people in the mountains that are capable of doing anything. I didn't say anything to Mag, but she sent word for me not to worry because there wasn't going to be anything happening to the three children. It didn't stop me losing sleep when they were out at night, but somehow, I believed if Mag said they would be safe, they would be.

"Jeremy had already shown signs of his purpose in life. When he was only ten, he was teaching the other children Bible stories. In his trips with Dot he came to be known as the preacher boy, and people started asking that he come with Dot and pray for them as Dot cared for their physical needs. Con was always there helping when he could, but otherwise just patiently waiting in the shadows. The three became quite famous for miles around, and people showed their appreciation by bringing us vegetables when they were in season and fresh meats in the winter months.

"The support we got from our neighbors, because they felt they owed the three children, made life easier for everyone.

"One cold snowy winter night, the three went across the ridge where an old woman lay dying. Her family knew she could not live, but they wanted Dot to ease her pain and Jeremy to pray with her that she might go in peace. These people of the mountains live rugged lives, and are not always in tune with what the rest of the world expects, but they have a steadfast faith in God and great respect for those who represent him here on earth.

"It was nearly three the next morning when I heard them making their way through the snow. I had kept a fire burning and they immediately moved toward the fire to try and bring some feeling back to their numb hands and feet. As they moved into the circle of light from the open fire, I could see their faces clearly for the first time and knew immediately something unusual had happened. The story they told me was that three drunk mountain boys blocked their path on the trail and demanded that Dot come with them and the boys keep going. They tried reasoning with them, but they were too full of moonshine to listen. One boy made a move toward Dot, and when he did, Jeremy stepped between them. The drunk mountain boy drew his knife and advanced toward Jeremy. Suddenly there was a loud noise and a snow slide came crashing down the mountain and across the trail. The boy with the knife was the only one caught in the slide and it carried him some thirty feet down the mountainside. They helped the other two boys dig him out of the snow, and Dot showed them how to pull his dislocated shoulder back in place. The three boys didn't give them any more trouble and left the area like the devil was right on their heels.

"This was the story Dot, Con, and Jeremy told, but the three mountain boys told a different tale. They didn't deny what they had tried to do and admitted they were very drunk, but from then on the story was different. The boy who had been carried down the mountain by the slide said, 'I heard it coming and looked up and there was that old witch Mag. She started the snow slide and what sounded like the cracking of underbrush was really that old witch jumping up and down laughing.' They told that story all over the mountain, and from that day on, not one person had the nerve to say one cross word to anyone of the three." Ellen remembered she had started to speak and Polly seemed to know what the question would be. She said, "Don't ask me if I believe that story. All I know is Mag said they would be safe and now I was sure of it. Mag had a tie to Jeremy that was beyond our understanding, and to try harming him in any way was risking her wrath."

Chapter XVIII

Polly sat quietly for quite some time and Ellen waited patiently for her to start her story again. Ellen wasn't sure if Polly needed to catch her breath or gather her thoughts, but she always started again with a new slant on the three people most important to her.

She started her new story telling Ellen how Jeremy, Con, and Dot had gradually taken over a large part of the orphanage operation.

With the information from her grandmother's book on herbs, reinforced by the help she had received from Mag, Dot had taken over as the resident health person. Polly stated that Con had gradually taken over the operation of the office and even at this young age was already a genius with figures. This had left Polly with time to monitor the staff and start new programs for the students.

"We figured that Jeremy was probably fourteen when he started conducting church services every Sunday morning. Con directed the children's choir and Jeremy preached. It started in the beginning as a service for the children and the staff, but the neighbors heard about it and started coming in. There were only a few at first, but when the rumors started spreading about the powerful words spoken by the young preacher, the congregation increased rapidly. The number of people coming in finally increased so it became necessary to leave the children in their attic bedrooms and turn over the great room to the outsiders.

"These services continued until the three of them left for college. It was a rough day for me when the time came for them to leave, because I had come to depend on them for so many things. Jeremy said, 'Don't worry, Miss Polly, you trained us and you can train others to take our place.' That never happened. You could search a lifetime to find a replacement for just one, but never for all three. Old Mag came over the day they left and she showed more emotion that day than I have ever seen from her. Mag admired and respected Dot and Con, but with Jeremy, it was always love. I guess love does not fully express how Mag felt, for the truth of the matter was she always worshipped Jeremy. You will also see that same expression in the eyes of many people in these mountains, because Jeremy introduced a lot of them to their savior and, like Mag, they look upon him as one of God's special people.

"Mag got Dot's promise that she would keep us informed and let me know I was to send all news on to her by the mailman. I faithfully relayed all news on to Mag and we didn't see much of her for a long time. People came by as they always had, bringing things they said Mag had instructed them to bring. Occasionally she would send a message that things were going well with Jeremy. It seemed she had a source of information concerning his welfare that we didn't have.

I hadn't seen Mag for what seemed like months, and one morning she came riding in here on Old Blue number two. Mag had to be in her nineties by now and that old mule looked like he would pass on any minute. Mag didn't say hello, how are you, or anything else in greeting, just what has Dot written about Jeremy. I told her the mailman hadn't arrived yet but the last letter I received, Jeremy was just fine. Mag said, 'I will wait for the mailman.' Mag didn't sit for more than five minutes at a time and then was up pacing the floor or looking to see if the mailman was coming up the mountain. When the mailman did arrive, Mag was off the porch before he could even get his car stopped. When he said there was no mail from Dot, I thought she would have a stroke. Mag said, 'Get your bonnet, Polly, we are going to Gatlinburg and call Dot.' It didn't make any difference to Mag that the mailman still had part of his route to finish; she had to go right then. They finally struck a deal; she would deliver the rest of his mail after he brought us back.

"Mag didn't ask if it was all right by me, but just told the mailman, 'We would bed him down at the orphanage and feed him the next morning,' before he went back down the mountain. It was obvious he didn't want to do what she asked, but also easy to see he was afraid not to. It was the first time I had been to Gatlinburg in years, but not much had changed. The year was about 1935 and from what I hear, it still hasn't changed much. Jeremy said the general store still is in operation at the fork of the main street and the river road. Also, the Mountain View Hotel still is in operation where the Cosby road forks off from the main road. I still remember the horses on the lawn of the hotel that people rented and rode up through town to the trails leading into the mountains. To a city girl it was just a wide place in the road, but coming out of the mountains as we were, it was rather intimidating.

"At the general store, I used the phone and was fortunate to get Dot right away. That was how I learned of Jeremy's accident and how Ruth had been killed. Dot said she was getting ready to write us that Jeremy had come out of the coma and was going to be fine. Of course, she meant he would be fine physically. Dot made it clear that Jeremy was taking Ruth's death very hard.

"I relayed to Mag what Dot was telling me, but she insisted she must talk to Dot. It was obvious Mag had never used a phone before because she yelled at the top of her voice. 'Dot, can you hear me?' The fellow tending the store laughed and said, 'If the operator was listening in on that call, she will never use that ear again.' Mag made Dot promise she and Con would take Jeremy home with them until he could work through this tragedy and that she would write every day so we would know how he was doing. After she hung up, Mag said, 'It will be a time of testing, but he will come through it a better man.'

"When we arrived back at the school, Mag dug deep into her apron pocket, found a gold coin and gave it to the mailman. She then let him know he must deliver all our mail from Dot without delay, and it was more an order than a request.

"Dot wrote every day, and I kept Mag informed, but if two days went by without me sending her the news, I could expect a visit from her and Old Blue. This went on for months, and all of us worried, but Mag was a total wreck. Mag never doubted Jeremy would work through his problems, but it seemed every hardship and every pain he suffered was felt by Mag.

"Things stayed this way for months and I wondered at times if they would ever get any better. Then one day Mag rode in here and, with one look at that mule, you knew she had driven Old Blue around the mountain in record time. Her feet didn't hit the ground before she said, 'What did Dot write about Ellen?'

"I replied, 'The mail isn't here yet, Mag, and I don't know what you are talking about.' She didn't answer, but just like she had done before, paced the floor for the next two hours as she waited.

"Dot's letter was in the mail and just as I expected, it was all about a girl named Ellen and also about the great opportunity Con had found for Jeremy. It was our first word about Jeremy as a college president and about you as a part of his life.

"For the first time in months, the strain that showed on Mag's face was gone, and she said, 'Now, he will be all right.' Her next words were strange, indeed, because she said, 'God has provided Jeremy a helpmate, and now he will fulfill his destiny.' After that Mag relaxed—it was as if she had shifted her burden to you and you were the answer."

When Polly paused, Ellen knew the time had come when she must ask the question that had been foremost in her mind. She had been afraid to hear the answer, but could wait no longer, and the words rushed from her mouth, in spite of her effort to hold them back.

"What did Mag say when she heard Jeremy was going into combat?" Ellen had finally asked the question and now she held her breath, dreading the answer.

"That was the same thing I had to know," said Polly, and I made my first and last trip around the mountain to visit Old Mag. "I rode with the mailman and that was the roughest six hours I have ever endured. I came back still wondering because I had no idea what her answer meant. Mag simply stated, 'This will be Jeremy's finest hour.'"

All afternoon as Ellen waited for Jeremy to return, she let the things Polly had told her run through her mind and thought of the questions she must ask Jeremy. That evening, after Jeremy had returned, while they sat talking before going to bed, Ellen asked Jeremy how he felt about the things Polly had told her about Mag, and especially her apparent ability to know things others did not know. Jeremy told her he could not answer her question because he didn't know, but he could not doubt Mag had contacts with a spiritual world others didn't have. Jeremy explained, "I believe in the Holy Spirit as God active in the world and in the affairs of men, so it is only reasonable to believe in a spiritual world closely connected to our physical world. There are some people like Mag who have a line of communication with this world. Most people don't have this open line of communication with the spiritual world that Mag and others have. Then again many of us may have this ability but have never tried to use it. This sets people like Mag apart from other people. We may not understand them, but we have no reason to doubt them."

Ellen waited until last to ask the question foremost in her mind because she was afraid to hear the answer. Ellen braced herself for the answer as she asked, "What did Mag mean when she said this will be Jeremy's finest hour?"

He answered, "It really doesn't matter. The only important thing is will it be God's finest hour in Jeremy's life." Ellen had her answer, but it told her nothing, because she had always known Jeremy's finest hour must always be God's finest hour.

Chapter XIX

It was just a few days until they would have to go back down the mountain and Jeremy would have to leave her and go on to face whatever lay in store for him. Jeremy had looked out that morning and said, "It looks like a great day for a long hike, so put on your best walking shoes." They left at about ten in the morning and Jeremy had told her only that they were going to visit Lou and it would be a five-mile hike both ways. They had been hiking for about two miles on a path running parallel to a fast-flowing creek when suddenly Jeremy stopped and pointed to a large poplar tree that had been cut down and made to fall across the creek and Ellen realized she was seeing her first foot log. The tree was edged on each bank between large rocks that kept it in place. The branches had been cut away and the top of the log had been crudely flattened by someone using an ax. Ellen would see other foot logs later that had ropes or vines strung on both sides for people to hold on to, but in this case, there were none. Jeremy told her to walk behind him with one hand on each shoulder, placing one foot in front of the other, and under no circumstances was she to look down. That first trip across a foot log was scary to say the least, but Ellen later would find such crossings a pleasure.

Standing on a foot log looking down into the fast-flowing water seemed to bring Ellen a sense of peace, and sighting a brown trout slowly moving upstream searching for food made her feel a part of the mountains.

That would all come later. Now she was just relieved to be on firm earth again and on their way following a path going the same direction on the opposite side of the creek. It seemed miles to Ellen before they left the path and headed up the mountain. The path here was steep and more rugged, but short. Ellen was thankful because she didn't think she could survive a lot of this type of hiking.

They came out of the woods into a very small clearing and were suddenly face-to-face with a very tall, slender woman. It was impossible to tell her age because her face was weather-beaten from years of hard living, and at the same time her body and the way she moved made her seem like someone still young. Jeremy simply said, "This is Lou."

She greeted Ellen like an old friend, saying, "Git up here on the porch where it is cool and set a spell." It didn't take Ellen long to realize Lou knew all about her because she was a close friend of Old Mag. They had not talked long before Jeremy said, "Lou, I would like for Ellen to see the still." This came as a surprise because it was the first time Ellen had heard about it. Lou did not reply but simply got up from her chair and started around the house with them following behind. It seemed to Ellen that a change had come over Lou—she marched as one embarked on a crusade. She approached a dilapidated shed a short distance in back of her cabin and as she swung back the door, it seemed a look of reverence crossed her face and she entered the shed with the look of one who was entering a sanctuary. For a few minutes everyone was silent as Ellen looked at a strange contraption constructed of what looked to Ellen like an old milk can, copper tubing, a galvanized tub, and coiled copper tubing. Then Lou slowly began to explain the parts and function of the still. "This is the boiler where the substance is heated and vaporized. This straight tube leads to the condenser where the vapor is run through this coiled copper tubing and the cold water in the condenser causes the vapor to become liquid. The coiled copper tubing is called the worm and the straight part at the end is the worm outlet, and from it the finished product is drained into containers." Ellen was sure she had received the simplest description on the working of a still that was possible, but to her it still seemed a little too complicated.

Lou closed the shed and they returned to the porch without saying a word.

They sat in silence for a few minutes and then Jeremy said, "Lou, why do you keep it?"

Lou replied, "It is a monument to my man and my oldest son. That still and two graves in that oak grove across the yard are all I have to remember them by."

"How did it happen, Lou?" asked Jeremy. "There had never been bad blood between your family and the revenuers in the past."

"Things changed, Jeremy. In the past, the officers didn't care if they caught anyone or not, but then a new group came in. This group was led by a killer and he wasn't satisfied just to destroy the stills, as the others had been, but seemed hell-bent on provoking a fight. It had always been easy to be gone before they arrived at the still site, because there were only two trails they could use to reach it. Both trails were always guarded and the alarm sounded, so it was possible to escape without a fight. Ned Potter was the lookout on the south trail and nobody knows what happened. He either went to sleep or they bought him off because they walked right in on my man and my Danny, and they never had no warning.

"We can never know what really happened, but some of the men think they shot Danny in the back before he ever went for his gun. The way things looked then, my man went crazy and sent three of them to hell before they finally got him. He was shot six times.

"Old Ned never did give a good explanation as to what happened. He claimed they snuck up on him and knocked him in the head, but some of the men said he was lying because there was not a big enough knot on his head to knock anybody out, not even Ned, and everybody knew his head was the weakest part about him. They talked about stringing him up and would have if I had encouraged them, but I don't believe in killing. If there had been other men in the family, a mountain feud might have started and the killing would have gone on for generations. There were only three of us—Amy, Jimmy, and me. Jimmy was only eight so we were facing some hard times.

"Amy decided to go to Sevierville and look for work even though she was only sixteen. My children could all read and write because I taught them just as my mother had taught me. My mother was an educated woman, who married a mountain man, and learned to love the mountains the same as she loved him.

"Amy got her a job in town waiting tables and sent enough money home for us to make out. We didn't hear anything about Ned for nearly six months and one of the men came by and told me he wasn't working or selling whiskey, but was spending money, so it wouldn't be long before he paid the price for violating the code of the hills. It wasn't more than three days after I got the message when I got up one morning and Jimmy was gone. It wasn't unusual for him to go out hunting before sunup, so when I checked and the hog rifle wasn't hanging over the mantle, I didn't give it another thought. He came in about ten and we had breakfast. He didn't bring in any game, but I hadn't heard a shot, so I figured he didn't find anything he wanted.

"About twelve noon the news arrived. The men said Ned had died that morning. They called it lead poisoning, a bullet square between the eyes. His wife said he got out of bed, walked out on his front porch to take a leak, and one shot was fired from a thicket about one hundred yards from his house. He fell like hundreds of hogs before him, uttering nary a squeal, and never knew what hit him. The big mystery is who could have done it? The men said your man and Danny were the only two people in these hills who could shoot like that and everybody knows it weren't them. There are those who say it was divine justice.

"Later in the day when I was alone, I took the hog rifle down from the pegs where it hangs and it smelled of fresh burnt powder. I hadn't heard a shot, but then Ned's house was too far off. I ran a cleaning wad down the barrel like I had seen my man do, just to make sure all evidence was gone. No one ever suspected. After Mag said, 'Vengeance is mine sayeth the Lord,' no man had nerve enough to even wonder.

"You are the only two people I have ever told this story, because if it is ever repeated, it will start a mountain bloodbath. Right now it can't affect Jimmy because he is in the Pacific fighting with the marines, but I hope and pray every night he will live to see the mountains again.

"If you are wondering why I am telling this story to the two of you, it is very simple. Jeremy is married to you and you are part of our family. You thought I knew so much about you, Ellen, because I am a friend of Mag's, but most that I found out I learned from Bruce."

Ellen didn't mind this part of her life running through her mind because it brought back memories of Bruce that warmed her heart. So she let all the memories engulf her as she became engrossed in the story as Lou told it.

"My old man never let any of the haulers come close to our place—fact is he met them as far away from here as possible. He even refused to let Danny go with him when he took them their load. He told me some are good men but a lot are not fit to associate with our children. Then one day he surprised me by saying, 'I have met a nice young man who would like to see more of the mountains, so fix something special for tonight because he will be visiting.'

"That night I met Bruce for the first time. I fixed a lot of country ham, redeye gravy, and cathead biscuits. The table was loaded with clay peas, mashed potatoes, corn, and polk greens fresh picked. After about thirty minutes, I started worrying where they would put the fresh peach cobbler I had fixed for dessert. Bruce hadn't said much, but that didn't bother me because when a man doesn't let talk interfere with his eating, he is complimenting the cook. Amy wasn't here when we started eating—she had gone to take Polly some things Mag had left for her and hadn't got back. I was sitting with my back to the kitchen door and wasn't aware that anyone had come in when suddenly Bruce stopped a biscuit in midair and sat staring with his mouth wide open. When he realized what he was doing, he turned red and apologized for staring, saying 'You look so much like my baby sister.' I turned and Amy was standing in the kitchen door framed by the evening sun as it was sinking over the ridge back of the house. I looked at Amy and back at Bruce, realizing immediately the fire between them would burn brighter than the sun streaming through her blonde hair.

"After we had finished eating, we sat on the front porch as the last of the evening sun faded across the mountains and Bruce told us about his baby sister with the golden hair and face of an angel. All the time Bruce talked and told us how much he loved his Ellen, I had the feeling he meant every word for my Amy as well. When I would look at Amy, I knew she was hanging on to each word knowing they were meant for her, and the look in her eyes let the joy in her heart shine out. From the very beginning you knew without a doubt two people had met that were meant to be one.

"Bruce didn't leave the next morning as planned, but remained an extra day. After that every trip he made, an extra day was spent here with Amy. They were married exactly one month from the day they first met. I will need to explain something here, Ellen, because you will not understand the kind of marriage I mean. We do not have a courthouse back here in the mountains and don't see a man of God very often, so people marry according to mountain custom. They let their intentions be known to those who have a right to know and then record the date in the family Bible. The couple then set up housekeeping and waited for a man of God to come through and bless their union. We see a man of God so seldom; it isn't unusual for the preacher to bless a union that has already been blessed by one or more children. You can find the marriage of Bruce Wallace and Amy Walker recorded in the large Bible on my writing table. Their marriage was never blessed by a man of God, but only by God himself.

"After they were married, Bruce spent more time here with Amy and then one day announced his intentions to quit hauling moonshine and move here permanently. His plan was to buy crafts from the mountain people and he and Amy take them to Knoxville and Asheville to be sold to gift shops. Some of the people were already selling to shops in Gatlinburg; the supply of good native crafts was greater than the few shops there could use. Bruce was sure a good customer base could be established in the larger cities and a better price could be obtained there.

"We had also decided as a family to no longer make the brew, but instead we would use our combined skills to produce woodcrafts and quilts for Bruce to sell. Those plans never came about because Bruce disappeared and for a few months we wondered what had happened. Then one day Amy received a letter from Bruce telling her he was in prison. From the very first, they both seemed to have a premonition that he would never live to return to the mountains. You know the rest. Bruce died, my man and my oldest son were killed, and Amy went to the city to work. The only thing I haven't told you is Amy came back home after two months because she was pregnant with Bruce's child.

"After Bruce, Jr., was born, she stayed here two months and then went back to Sevierville to work. Amy sent us all the money we needed and came home on a regular schedule. It was when she came home for the boy's fourth birthday that she brought home a very polished gentleman who was ten years her senior. He wanted Amy to marry him, but she had refused until he came to the mountains and saw for himself where she was from. He told me he had never doubted what he would find because a person like Amy could only come from people with class.

"Amy was lucky she had loved two first-rate men and they both had loved her. Her new husband was not only a real gentleman, but also a very rich lumberman. My grandson goes by his father's name, but he has had every advantage his new father could give him. He is about thirteen now and a wonderful boy. I know you would like to meet him and you can be sure both Amy and the boy's new Father would welcome you to their home in Asheville." Jeremy never got to see Bruce, Jr., because they didn't have time to visit before he was shipped overseas.

They were leaving and Lou had walked with them to the edge of the woods as if she were reluctant to see them go, and suddenly brought a letter from her apron pocket saying, "Preacher, I must read you this letter. It is from Jimmy."

> *Dear Mom:*
>
> *These jungles here are hot and very uncomfortable and no place to have to live. I am thankful every day for the kind of life I lived in the mountains. It is making it possible for me to survive and to help others survive. These boys from the city can't understand how I can know where the enemy is and can keep them from getting caught in an ambush. I tell them it isn't any different from listening for the movement of squirrel, deer, turkey, and bear, but they have no way to understand.*
>
> *I was called up front yesterday where a company was pinned down by sniper fire. They led me to a small clearing where I could see three bodies just off the path. They told me the first man had been shot and his buddy had tried to save him and had also been picked off. The third man was a medic who had gone to give them aid.*
>
> *I knew immediately what had happened. These men were new to combat and hadn't learned you never go to the aid of a man who has been shot by a sniper until you first eliminate the sniper. When the sniper got the first man he had his gun zeroed in on that spot, so when the next two stepped into his line of fire, all he had to do was squeeze the trigger.*
>
> *After I had surveyed the sight, I was sure the sniper could not be firing from ground level, but was in one of the larger trees on the other side of the clearing. They always use natural foliage as camouflage, so*

finding him would not be easy. I used the method I always used when hunting squirrel. I let my eyes follow slowly each limb and the tree trunk looking for an unusual formation or bump and then watch that one spot waiting for movement. It is easier spotting squirrel because eventually he will move his tail. These snipers are very patient, and many times the only way to spot one is waiting for him to move his rifle. I finally thought I had him spotted, but he seemed to be flat against the front side of the trunk which was very unusual. I had one of our men put a helmet on a long stick and hold it just where it could be seen above the underbrush. Fortunately for us, he had never seen any American westerns and moved his gun for a shot. As soon as his gun was in place to shoot, I had my target. I squeezed off one shot and his gun fell to the ground, but he remained in place. The lieutenant in charge ordered his men to stay undercover saying he may have another gun. I knew he was dead so I walked on across the clearing. When I was close enough, I could see why he hadn't fallen—he was roped to the front of the trunk and left there until he was killed or starved. We cut him down and there was a small hole right between the eyes. At least he had not suffered. A young boy who had not been in combat long walked to one side and lost his breakfast. He then asked me how can you do this and then calmly walk away; if he only knew the turmoil that churns inside. I ask myself the same question, but then as I watch three young boys placed in body bags, I know there is no other way. I did not make a choice; the choice was made for me. All I can do is use the skills I have to save as many as possible.

Four men died in this jungle clearing today, but many more will die in the next few weeks. When the telegrams are delivered, there are mothers, fathers, sisters, brothers, wives, children, and friends who will die inside, and that death will stay with everyone it touches for years to come.

I know that God can read my heart, and he knows I do not take these lives because I hate. They are our enemy, but, like us, they are the victims of something too great for me to understand. I can only pray the lives I have saved will be balanced against the lives I have taken, and God, in his divine love, will forgive me. I love you and my heart yearns for the mountains.

Love,
Jimmy

Lou paused, folded the letter, and took a deep breath before she trusted herself to speak. Her voice was a cry for help as she uttered the words, "Jeremy, what can I do? Is my son doomed to hell?" As Ellen listened to Jeremy answer

Lou, she more fully understood why he felt he had no choice but to go into combat. She was finally able to understand why he felt the men in combat need someone to keep them in touch with God. Jeremy had an answer for Lou that Ellen felt was simple and convincing. "The things that happen in combat are not the sin. The sin happened long before, and is the accumulated sin of all of us. Paul wrote, 'The wages of sin is death and war is the payment for our sin because we have all failed to live according to the teachings of our Lord and Savior.' The men who do the killing feel more guilt, but they are no guiltier in the sight of God than the rest of us."

Jeremy seemed to speak to the mountains as he softly spoke his next remarks, "He lived before us the life we are supposed to live, and only when we live that life will we be free from the suffering and heartache that we experience." Ellen was totally unprepared for what happened next. Not a word was spoken, but Jeremy and Lou joined hands and each one took one of her hands. They knelt there by a fallen log and Ellen had no choice but to kneel with them. Jeremy began to pray, and as he prayed, Lou joined in. Ellen had experienced before the shouting and loud demonstrations of emotion in Church of God meetings, but this was different. To Ellen, it was more like two people talking with a mutual friend, and it became for her a very moving experience. Ellen recalled a conversation she once overheard between two elderly ladies. One had remarked, "When Dr. Jeremy Grimes prays, he takes you to the foot of the cross." Ellen wondered if perhaps now she understood.

As they left and made their way down the mountain, Ellen was very quiet as she reflected on what had happened. When Jeremy asked what was wrong, Ellen convinced him she was just fatigued and would be fine after a night's rest. Ellen decided then she must get her emotions under control and be in a happy frame of mind until Jeremy left.

Chapter XX

It had rained for two days and Ellen was satisfied just to sit by the window and relax. The trip to see Lou had been enjoyable but also very tiring. Ellen had been reading and Jeremy was finishing some last-minute paperwork in preparation for leaving. It seemed that time was rushing by faster than ever as the time drew near for his departure. They were spending these last minutes together before an open fire, in the fireplace, and even when they sat and did nothing, time still seemed to fly by.

Ellen had finally consented to go visit Dot for two weeks rather than go to Oglethorpe with Jeremy. It was what Jeremy wanted because he knew he would have very limited time to be with her and did not wish her spending time alone in a hotel room. Jeremy also felt it would be easier for Ellen to get used to being alone if she was with Dot. That word alone made Ellen face a reality that, up until now, she had kept buried and not allowed to become a part of conscious thought.

Before they left the mountains, Jeremy gave Miss Polly a sizable donation and told her if at any time things became difficult financially to contact Ellen or Dot because they both had access to money. Jeremy also instructed Ellen to make sure she contacted H.T. if the orphanage ever needed anything.

Their only transportation out of the mountains was with the mailman in his old Ford Model A. After that ride, Ellen found the overnight trip in a crowded train car comfortable by comparison. Con and Dot met them at the station, and the first thing Ellen requested was a hot tub to soak in. She let the warm water soothe her aching body and calm her racing mind. Ellen stayed in the tub a long time and marveled that most of the world took such luxuries for granted. Ellen's next thought shocked her as she wondered how many young men were shivering in foxholes tonight and dreaming of the day when they might once again enjoy such pleasure.

Jeremy had to leave after two days, and Ellen knew she would never forget the anguish that showed in the faces of Dot, Con, and Jeremy. She stood and wondered why she had not recognized the tie that bound these three together before now. They were a family and had been all their lives. Three children, and now three adults who had never known sister, brother, mother, or father—all they had ever known was each other. It made Ellen feel richly blessed and loved as never before to be included in such a family. Knowing that Jeremy was leaving, she was fully confident she would always be loved and cared for. It made his leaving even harder for her because once again, Jeremy would be alone.

Even though Jeremy would be alone once more with only his God and his mission in life to sustain him, Ellen was confident this would be sufficient. She refused to let the thought that she might never see him again become a part of her thinking. Ellen talked only of the future and the life they would have together when he returned. Their marriage had started as a convenience for both of them, but had become one of mutual love and respect. It had happened step-by-step: need, desire, passion, friendship, and then an all-consuming love without reservations.

Jeremy left telling her he would call the following night after he and H.T. concluded their business. Jeremy also planned to call every night from Oglethorpe and any place else he might find himself up until he shipped out of New York.

Ellen retired early the night after Jeremy left, and Dot, sensing she didn't want company, left her alone with her thoughts. It was a long night and Ellen slept very little. Ellen knew she had come a long way from the world where she grew up, but doubted that night she was strong enough to face the trying times ahead without Jeremy.

For the next week, Ellen was with Dot continually and Dot did all she could to keep her too busy to think. Jeremy called as he said he would, but there wasn't anything that could fill the empty place in Ellen's heart, or erase the fear that gripped her. Dot and Con took Ellen home after a week, and there she faced the reality that this was a battle she would face alone. Friends tried to help, but Ellen found, alone in bed at night, there wasn't anything that could help her escape from the fear that gripped her. Before Jeremy left, Ellen, by sheer willpower, refused to let the idea she might never see him again enter her conscious thoughts, but now this reality gripped her and there was no escape. H.T. did everything he could to keep her occupied. Ellen even suspected he planned events at school that were not necessary just to keep her around people. Gradually, Ellen was able to resume a life that was close to normal, but a life that was never free from a constant anxiety that never let up.

Jeremy called as long as he was in the United States, which was almost two months. Both Jeremy and Ellen learned very quickly that the armed forces moved slowly, which was extremely nerve-racking for Jeremy. Finally, there came a period of time without calls or letters and Ellen knew he was on his way. Those days and nights without news brought on new worries because, like everyone else, Ellen knew the losses at sea were high.

Chapter XXI

The period of waiting when there was no word from Jeremy was worse than the days that would follow when Ellen knew he was in danger. After two weeks of no news, there would begin the period that Ellen remembered as the letter-writing years. Ellen could not possibly remember all the letters that Jeremy wrote, but there were some she would never forget. Some she remembered because they gave her an inside view of what was happening that most people never knew.

March 2, 1944

Dearest Ellen:

Finally we have arrived. The crossing was free of danger, but from what I can hear, this is the exception and not the rule. An ocean voyage on a ship completely blacked out is anything but enjoyable. The men are bored out of their minds, and as long as it is light enough, do nothing but gamble. I dislike gambling very much, but in this case, it is the only way they can maintain their sanity.

Now that we are in a staging area, I had hoped things would change, but they haven't. It is all hurry up and wait. It is hard not to get frustrated, but it doesn't help. Moving such a large body of men and all the supplies they will need is a vast undertaking.

To say that I miss you is an understatement, because you have become the most important person in my life. It is not unusual for something to happen during the day that will make me think I must tell Ellen about this tonight. This though is always devastating and leaves me depressed for hours. I dread seeing the sun go down because the nights without you are hard for me to bear. Without you my work is all I have left, and it is all that keeps me going. Darling, I love you more than I can ever say, and I live for the day when I can hold you once more.

All my love,
Jeremy

Even now as Ellen remembered that letter, she still had difficulty thinking of war as being boring. Ellen had talked to many returning veterans after the war and they had all said the boredom of waiting for things to develop had been difficult.

March 10, 1944

Dearest Ellen:

Finally the waiting is over—the troops have been moved into position to back up General Mark Clark's Fifth Army on Anzio Beach. This will give me more work because now I can visit the troops in the field and also visit the wounded who are hospitalized. We are still suffering some casualties on the beach from artillery fire, but nothing nearly as great as will be sustained once the drive on Rome is under way.

I have spent my time with the ground forces and I know what they are called on to face, but I know very little about the air force.

I have asked an air force officer, whose stay in the hospital is over, to see if he can get permission for me to go on a bombing mission as an observer. Men who have suffered physical wounds are the same whether they are infantry or air force, but I need to know what causes mental breakdown, and here there would be a difference.

Enough about this day—I should be telling you how much I love you. There is never a day, never a minute that I do not miss you. I live for the day when we will once again be together; knowing that you feel the same makes life bearable. My hardest job, so far, has been trying to counsel men who have received "Dear John" letters. It is difficult to convince a man life is still worth living when the woman he loves writes, "I no longer love you enough to wait for your return." That burden, added to what they face here at times, becomes more than they can bear. I know I shouldn't burden you with these problems, but then again, having you to share these things with makes the load lighter. That could be the best definition of true love, two people facing the problems of life as a team.

Ellen, I thank God every day for sending you to me. Without you, my life would have been over. We have, with God's help, done much good, and if it is his will, even greater things are ahead.

> *With all my love,*
> *Jeremy*

Ellen realized she was getting Jeremy's letters days after very important events had taken place. Many of the things Jeremy wrote about Ellen had heard about on the radio or seen in news reels, but hearing about them from Jeremy made them more personal.

March 20, 1944

Dearest Ellen:

I miss you more than you can ever know. If I were not so busy, the loneliness would drive me out of my mind. It is even worse for the infantry who spend day after day in the rain and mud, seldom bathing or getting to sleep in a dry bed. This causes some resentment toward the Air Corps, who fly over on their way to bomb a target and then fly back over as they return to their base and a hot shower, hot food, and a dry bed. Some things have happened lately that have given the infantry a different perspective where the flyboys are concerned. The German resistance at Casino had been deadly. They were using Casino Abbey as a spotter tower to direct their artillery fire, and with good results. The top brass were reluctant to bomb a Catholic monastery first built in 529 AD, knowing the backlash would be enormous. In the end, they had no choice because too many men were dying. The decision would not have been hard for me to make because there isn't a temple, mosque, tabernacle, or cathedral worth one life. These structures were built by man, but these men were created by God. If it would save one life, I would personally drop a bomb on the Vatican City.

The decision to bomb was carried out by B-26, B-25, and B-24 aircraft, and the Abbey and the town are in rubble. To help relieve the backlash, if it does occur, the B-26 group used only Catholic bombardiers who volunteered for the mission. The pilot who gave me my information said his bombardier was not only Catholic, but also Italian-American. Do not tell this to anyone, but if it does come out and the men who made the decision are threatened in any way, take my letter to H.T. and he will use influence to help them.

As usual, I seem to be using my letters to you to build my morale or to help solve some problem. You know you are everything to me, and without you, I would be completely lost. I want to hold you in my arms

*so much they actually ache along with my heart. I live each day only
because I know one day we will be together again.*

*Love,
Jeremy*

April 10, 1944

My Darling:

*I waited until now to write about it, but I did get to go on a
mission with the B-26 group about two weeks ago. My commanding
officer objected at first, but was told the German supply lines had
been cut and they were lacking in ammunition, so it would be an
easy mission. What they didn't tell him was the Germans usually used
what they had and concentrated on as many flights as they could. We
happened to be one of the flights that got the concentration of fire.*

*I was observing things through a Plexiglas observation bubble
mounted on top of the plane just over the radio room. I was totally
engrossed as the shells burst leaving large black clouds and the planes
wove back and forth between them like a runner carrying a football in
an open field. Suddenly the tail gunner screamed over the intercom he
is going to ram us. His voice relayed his fear and suddenly I realized
why when a burning plane came into my line of sight. A plane in
formation behind us had received a direct hit and resembled a flaming
blowtorch. The plane was completely out of control. I froze, unable to
move, as the plane came up beside us, rolled completely over the top of
our plane, and down on the other side. I was not able to see the plane
from my position, as it spun on toward earth, but the ones who could,
said there were no parachutes. The navigator told me it would be very
unusual for anyone to get out of a plane hit in that way. He said, "One
minute the men will be tossed about like bowling pins, and at other
times the force will pin them to the floor sides or ceiling of the plane
and they will be unable to move." Now I will understand if a flier who
has come unglued tells me I wake up at night screaming. I had one boy
tell me he slept next to one fellow who would dream at night and end
up bailing out of his bunk.*

*These boys joke about things that happen, but they never mention
the most obvious. There were six men who died in that plane, and once
the crews gave their report at debriefing, they went to chow. It seems
they talk about funny things; the others are blocked from their minds.
This is the only way to cope, but some day these things must be faced,
and professional help will be needed. H.T. and I have discussed this*

and I am sure he is preparing that help. If it is God's will, I hope to be a part of that work.

Ellen, you need not worry about me being in danger again because I was told without asking I had made my last mission.

This has been an unusual letter for a man to write to a woman he loves, but it seemed I had no choice. I had never looked death in the eye before, and it seems to influence the way I approach living. There is a new urgency in the things I must do, because I realize as never before tomorrow is a promise that may not be kept.

Ellen, you are very dear to me and this brush with death has made me see more fully how much you have enriched my life. More than ever before, I am sure that God sent you into my life when I needed you most, and you have fulfilled that part of your life's purpose to its fullest. There is no way I can ever tell you how much good you have done by just being a part of my life. You have been my strength and my inspiration, and your love has been my greatest.

Love,
Jeremy

As this letter ran through her mind, it brought cold chills, just as it had through the years. Ellen felt the first time she read the letter that Jeremy was having a premonition of what was ahead. Reviewing the words of that letter, even now, Ellen remembered how powerless she felt as she faced the inevitable.

April 23, 1944

Dear Ellen:

General Sherman was right, "War is hell." I have been moving from the frontline mash units to the larger hospitals in the rear trying to keep in touch with the wounded as long as possible. It isn't necessary to see the actual fighting to get a clear picture of the horror—it shows in the eyes of these men who have been there.

I try to spend as much time as I can with the men who are not in the hospital but are getting ready to move into combat. Many are seasoned veterans, but a great many are untested in combat. These men dread what they face, but their greatest fear is not being able to cast aside their fears and face the task ahead.

Once the drive begins, which is bound to be soon, I hope I can move with the men and stay as close to the fighting as possible. My superiors tell me to stay in the rear, that all wounded will eventually arrive there, but some are sure to die before they reach the rear and I find it hard to think of even one boy dying without someone to hold his hand and pray.

Ellen, you may not get my letters on a regular schedule once the troops start moving. I pray I will not be too busy to write, but I am sure I shall be.

I love you,
Jeremy

May 28, 1944

Darling Ellen,

You probably know the details about the drive in Italy, possibly better than I do. Trying to cover the work is almost impossible. I find sleep impossible regardless of how tired I may be. There is a never-ending stream of wounded and they need someone who can give them hope. This running battle as the Germans try to escape from Italy will go on for months. This is going to be some of the bitterest fighting of the war. At times I wonder if it would not be better to let them go, but common sense tells us it would even be harder to fight them on German soil.

War is very unfair because it takes those most qualified and gives them the most dangerous jobs. These are the ones always in the eye of the storm.

John was one such person. He was captain of his high school track team and good at many other sports. When the drive started on Rome, he was given the job of point man. This is the man who will be out front several hundred yards ahead of the main body. It is his job to make sure he finds the enemy before his forces fall into a trap. This means he will see the enemy before everyone else. The point guard's survival depends on his ability to see the enemy before they see him.

John was brought into the hospital this morning. He was wounded just a few miles from Rome. He will be in the hospital for a few weeks, but when better, will be returned to the front.

Things have eased up a little and I am getting more rest, but we need to be closer to the men who are fighting. If these men ever needed spiritual guidance and a strong faith, it is now. I have been trying to get my commander to let me work closer to where the men are fighting. I am sure they need someone to talk with about their faith, and there are sure to be a few who need to know Christ as a personal savior. It takes time to change anything in the service, but I will eventually get my way.

They are increasing the staff of chaplains here at the hospital. I am not sure what it means, but I hope it will mean I can eventually do my work with the men who are doing the fighting. It is still my belief that our job is to give spiritual guidance and hope to those who are still fighting, as well as the wounded.

Pray for me, Ellen, that I might make the next few months glorify God.

All my love,
Jeremy

June 14, 1944

Dear Ellen:

Finally I am doing what I feel is badly needed. I am following the troops as they drive up the Poe Valley into Northern Italy. I am not close enough to be in danger, so don't worry about me. I do get a chance to see many wounded as they are brought back from the front. Groups are also pulled back and others take the lead so they can get some rest. These are the times when I feel I am doing the greatest good. It gives me the opportunity to conduct services for these troops and also to counsel with those who need to talk.

I met an ambulance recently as we moved toward the front. I had my driver stop so I could talk with the men. There was a sergeant in the ambulance that I had met in the training at Oglethorpe. He asked that I come over and talk with him. He told me things were well with him, but he just wanted to make sure I saw something about five miles farther down the road. He told me it wouldn't take long—he had passed through it as he was going forward just before he was wounded. The sergeant told me there was a forest just about one mile to the right side of the road and to have my driver drive me over there and I would see a sight I would never forget.

About five miles down the road, as we moved toward the front, a stand of large trees covering several acres appeared on our right. I told my driver to take the dirt road leading in that direction and we would see what the sergeant was talking about. He was correct. What I saw will be a part of my memory as long as I live. A German panzer unit had been hiding there waiting to ambush the American infantry forces. Intelligence had relayed the information to the B-26 bomb group flying off the island of Sardinia, and they had bombed earlier that morning.

The Germans were caught completely by surprise and were totally destroyed. The planes had carried fragmentation bombs and the destruction was beyond description. The bark was literally stripped from the trees, and the mechanized vehicles made it impossible to get close, but we were close enough to smell the burning flesh and recognize the burned bundles under and around the vehicles as bodies.

Your feelings are mixed at such a sight, and it is easy to forget these are enemy soldiers, and I found myself praying for the men who had died there.

After the initial shock, I thought of the American infantry and what would have happened if they had walked into the trap waiting for them.

I can only pray the men on the planes that dropped those bombs will never know the extent of their work this morning. I know the men of the air force think about what takes place, because I once had a flier tell me, "I know what happens when the bombs fall, but we can't see it, and it is better that way."

Ellen, I am satisfied with the work I am now doing because I feel I make a difference in the lives of others. I realize this does little to relieve your anxiety, but be happy for me and know, regardless of the outcome, this is what I was meant to do.

Ellen, please keep these letters for me. I know I will never forget what I have written, but I want to read them again later so the tragedy of war, I hope to one day tell the next generation, will be just as real then as it is today. Those of us here can only imagine the daily grief and worry endured by wives, children, mothers, and fathers of the men who fight here. It is my daily prayer that one day we will come to our senses and live as Christ taught us to live.

Darling, I can only repeat how much I love and miss you, and hope by repeating it, you will come to know the depth of my love.

Eternally yours,
Jeremy

June 30, 1944

Dearest Ellen:

When I think of all the things I see every time I get close to the front, I can only imagine the things the men see who remain in the thick of the fight. The front line was stalled recently and was pinned down by German eighty-eights. Suddenly we were up front closer than my sergeant was supposed to take me. He pulled our jeep off the road and we joined a small group of men in a hastily built bunker. The captain in charge informed us he had called for an air strike and it was *due any minute. He said the guns were only about two miles ahead, so we could expect to feel and hear the bombs when they explode.*

We watched as the planes came over and the German guns quit firing at us and directed their fire at the planes. The shells were bursting in big black clouds all around the planes. We could see the bombay doors open and the bombs streaking toward the earth. The thought came to me, how frightened the men must be watching those bombs falling toward them. Suddenly one of the planes burst into flames, a shell had exploded under the right engine. The plane started spinning out of control. The thought came to me, I have seen this before, and they cannot get out. Then suddenly the plane became stable and parachutes started to open. We counted as each parachute opened, but when we reached five for a few seconds nothing happened, and I could hear myself praying, "God, let there be one more." A cheer started in my throat, but just as suddenly died there. The pilot had stayed at the controls long enough for his crew to clear the aircraft, but too long to save his own life. With his parachute flaming behind him, he plunged to his death. The burning fuel had ignited his parachute.

I looked at the other men and was amazed to see a veteran infantry sergeant with tears running down his cheeks. I found myself repeating the words of Jesus as recorded in John 15:13, "Greater love hath no man than this that a man lay down his life for his friends." I know that I shall never again doubt the power of God's love, for here at the very gates of hell, God's divine love lives in the hearts of his people.

The apostle Paul wrote to the church at Rome the following words recorded in Romans 8:38–39, "For I am persuaded that neither death, nor life, nor angels, nor principalities, nor powers, nor things present, nor things to come, nor height, nor depth, nor any other creature shall be able to separate us from the love of God, which is in Christ Jesus our Lord."

All my love,
Jeremy

July 20, 1944

My Darling:

I know it has been a while since I have written, but I have been on the move. I am constantly on the move because our troops are still chasing the Germans as they retreat out of Italy hoping to reach home where they will join their comrades in their last ditch stand. The British and French forces are also fighting alongside our troops, and if we can stop these Germans escaping from Italy, it will make the final fighting to take Germany much easier. The Germans retreat and blow up all bridges behind them and this slows down our forces. The air force is now using a new tactic—they bomb all bridges before the German troops reach them. Their route up the Poe Valley on their way to the Brenner Pass won't have a bridge left on any major highway. Our troops, of course, will leave their pontoon bridges in place where they can.

You will never know how some small thing can bring a ray of sunshine into an otherwise dreary day. We were crossing a river yesterday on a temporary bridge as the MASH unit was moving to get closer to the troops. As our jeep crossed, I just happened to look down and on the other side of a pontoon. I read Dempster Brothers, Knoxville, Tennessee. It was like a letter from home saying you are not forgotten, we are also fighting.

There is a battalion of Japanese Americans fighting their way up the Poe Valley. They are fighting hard and many have made the supreme sacrifice in an effort to prove their allegiance to their adopted land. I pray their many sacrifices will make it easier for the American people to come to grips with their hatred for all Japanese. My darling, I pray for the day when this madness will end and I can hold you in my arms once more. You brought fullness to my life when I thought it was over. The greatest sorrow I feel is for the many young men who will die here never knowing the joy of a dream fulfilled or having found the joy of true love.

Good night for now, my love; I will rest hoping to dream of you.

I will love you forever,
Jeremy

August 15, 1944

Dearest Ellen:

I am sitting in the chaplain's study at the hospital, far from fighting. I was called back from following the troops temporarily because things are going to be too much for the regular staff to handle.

The invasion of Southern France started two hours ago and in another hour or so we will be filled to capacity with wounded. Just how many wounded we have will depend on how well the invasion goes, but by the time you get this letter you will probably know more than I do.

August 17, 1944

Darling Ellen, as you can see, I had to stop writing and now, two days later, I can finally finish this letter. I thought I would have plenty of time to finish before the wounded started coming back from the beach, but I didn't plan or expect wounded from the Air Corps. The B-26 bomb group on Sardinia had six planes crash on takeoff and only two crews survived. These wounded and dead kept us busy until the other wounded arrived from the landing, so it has taken two days for me to get back to writing you.

I will never become hardened to what is happening here—men are not created to kill and be killed. God truly loves us or he would have turned from us long ago.

You will recall I wrote about John, who was wounded before he reached Rome. He is back with us again. John returned to his unit just before they were pulled out of Italy to make the landing in France. He reached France, but he walked ashore. The landing craft he was in struck a mine and John made the beach with only the handle of his shovel. He is not as seriously wounded as before, and will be sent back to the front shortly.

I will be here for a while yet, but will eventually be allowed to return to the fighting troops. Life is much easier here, but I can never be at peace unless I am near those who need to hear God's message the most. Until we meet again, my love, I hold you in my heart.

Love,
Jeremy

September 15, 1944

Darling Ellen:

As you can tell, I am still at the hospital, but not for much longer. I have been told I can go back to the frontline troops tomorrow. This is a great relief, because I feel very strongly this is where I need to be.

I told you before: John would be sent back to the front. He didn't stay long, but came back to the hospital yesterday. He was wounded somewhere in France. He didn't see Rome, and will not see Paris, because this time they are going to send him home. He is lucky. I know it sounds strange to say a man is lucky when he is going home minus one eye and a body full of metal he will carry the rest of his life. But he is lucky because most people wounded as many times as he has been, go home in a bag. You will hear some say this war has been an experience they will always cherish, but let me tell you, they are the ones who never fought it. War is stupid, senseless, and without any redeeming qualities.

I must close for now, my darling, and I hold you in my heart. If it were not for my love for you, and my friends, it would be very easy to give up on all mankind.

War is that horrible, but I know it is God's world, and his love will conquer.

Love,
Jeremy

September 30, 1944

My Love:

We have stopped, because the roads must be made passable before we can go on. This letter may be short because we are not usually stalled for long. We are constantly on the move so you will not receive as many letters as I have written in the past. As I sit here in the jeep, I can see the Alps Mountains in the distance.

I cannot be sure how many miles away they are because the day is clear and when your vision is not obstructed by the landscape, it is possible to see for miles. It is only September, but the higher mountain peaks are covered with snow.

I see a mountain chalet far in the distance, and I sit here dreaming. I can see us inside curled up snug and warm before a roaring fire enjoying a second honeymoon. We can let this be our plan once this hell is behind us.

Just as I expected, things are starting to move up ahead, so we will be on the move soon. I will give this letter to someone headed for the rear, and you should receive it soon.

All my love,
Jeremy

Ellen's letter, dated September 30, 1944, was the shortest letter Jeremy had ever written her, but it was among the ones she always remembered, because it was his last.

Chapter XXII

Every morning for over a month Ellen went to the school post office, and every day she returned home feeling lower than the day before. She tried to feel positive, but in her heart, Ellen had always had to suppress the feeling Jeremy would not come home.

The morning was damp and dark, and it seemed the light of day would never shine through. Ellen was standing at the front window just waiting for the time to come when she could go for the morning mail. Her heart seemed to stop beating as she saw H.T. coming up the front walk accompanied by an army officer. Ellen knew the procedure and the officer's mission could only mean one thing. The officer was a colonel in the Chaplains Corps, and he brought the news that Jeremy had been killed in action.

Ellen made it to the door to let them in, but never remembered how she did it or what she had done or said. It would be later that H.T. would tell her what the colonel had said, because not one word had registered. It did not really matter at the time because she was suffering too much pain for his words to bring comfort.

It would be months before the words the colonel had spoken would have any meaning or bring any comfort. H.T. had quoted the colonel as saying Major Jeremy Grimes brought honor to himself, to his country, and to the God he served. Ellen was especially moved by the statement that Jeremy had brought honor to his God, because she knew, this being the case, it would also have been Jeremy's finest hour, just as Mag had predicted.

Ellen could not remember many details about that day; she did remember the chaplain didn't stay long. Ellen could remember that she and H.T. sat alone in the quiet house and said very little. The one thing Ellen remembered most vividly was looking at H.T. and wondering if her face revealed the excruciating pain she saw revealed in his.

H.T. had already called Dot before coming to the house and she and Con arrived about two hours later. It was only after Dot arrived that Ellen lost control of her emotions. Ellen lay on her bed with Dot holding her head and cried until she thought there could be no more tears. Con stood motionless, never shedding a tear or saying a single word. This bothered H.T. because he knew how Con was suffering, and he told Dot if Con didn't give in to his emotions, he might never be able to put it behind him.

Dot told H.T. not to worry, that Con would give in to his emotions, but only when the two of them were alone. Ellen would know what she meant when later that night she could hear his cries of pain as Dot tried late into the night to console him. Now that Con had only one person left in his life that was close to him, Ellen feared what might happen if he ever lost Dot. Ellen made a pledge to Jeremy that night to try and fill the void in Con's life. Ellen knew there was no way she could ever mean as much to Dot and Con as Jeremy had meant, but she knew for herself, as well as for them, she must try.

Ellen went home with Dot and Con and each one tried in their own way to cope with their sorrow and to be there for the others when needed. H.T. never failed to call each day and made frequent trips into the office to talk with Con. Ellen was certain most of this business could have been conducted by phone, but that H.T. was making an effort to keep them busy and their minds occupied. There was no doubt in anyone's mind that Con's work was all that ensured his sanity. Con was such a deep thinker that once his mind was focused on a problem, it was impossible for him to focus on anything else. In business, this was Con's greatest asset, but in everyday living, it could be his greatest liability.

Chapter XXIII

After Ellen had been at Dot and Con's for about six weeks, H.T. came for a visit and Ellen could see immediately that he had something to discuss. The first time they were alone, H.T. asked Ellen if she were ready to attend a memorial service for Jeremy. The school had just finished building a new chapel and the board of trustees had voted to name it the Jeremy K. Grimes Memorial Chapel. Ellen dreaded the thought that she might lose control of her emotions in a large group of people, but knew waiting would not make it any easier, so it was decided the service would be two weeks from the following Sunday.

Ellen felt it was time she vacated the president's house so they could start looking for someone to take over as president, but when she suggested it to H.T., he said no, not for at least six months. The board had decided to wait for this length of time and she would continue to work for the school and live in the president's house. If she were agreeable to this plan, she would draw a salary as an employee of the school. Ellen's duties would be much the same as before, assisting H.T. and the dean in the school's operation. H.T. said he did not want to be rushed because they needed an exceptional person if the school was to maintain the high standards Jeremy had set.

Ellen had seen the new chapel building, for the outside work had been finished for some time, but she was not prepared for the elaborate finish work she found inside. Ellen knew the expensive furnishings, the artistic use of wood trim, and the large pipe organ were not part of the original plan. Ellen learned later these changes were financed by H.T. He had stated, "This chapel will be the focal point of the school and it is only fitting that it be a worthy tribute to the man responsible for what we have here."

Ellen was surprised again when she saw the large assembly of people gathered to pay tribute to Jeremy. The Chaplains Corps was represented by several high-ranking officers, but the most impressive to Ellen was the large number of enlisted personnel in attendance. These men were not long out of the hospital, because it was evident they were all wounded in some manner. Some were on crutches, some had an arm in a cast, or sling, while others seemed unsteady as they walked to their seats. The most emotional time for Ellen was after everyone was seated—six men were rolled into the service in wheelchairs—for it brought back the things Jeremy had written about the horrors of war. Ellen felt for the first time she fully understood why at times Jeremy seemed depressed. These were the ones he had wanted to comfort.

Ellen knew at a memorial service there was usually a picture of the person being remembered, but she was not prepared for what she saw. On an easel was a large oil portrait of Major Jeremy K. Grimes in full dress uniform, complete in every detail, even to the medals he had earned in combat. A bronze plaque beneath the picture read, "Commissioned by H.T. Thompson." H.T. had not consulted Ellen about this, but she understood—it was his tribute to a friend. The portrait would hang in the entrance to the chapel so that future generations might know the man responsible for the many opportunities offered them in this place.

Ellen would learn later the wounded men who were there were the men Jeremy had served. H.T. had made it possible for them to attend by furnishing his private railcar to transport them from the hospital. When the service ended, the people passed in front of Jeremy's portrait as a final farewell. The wheelchairs went first, and the most moving tribute was when one young soldier had his attendant turn his wheelchair facing the picture, then gripping both arms of the chair, forced himself to a standing position and stood at attention long enough to salute. At that moment, Ellen needed all her strength to control her emotions.

After everyone had left, H.T. informed Ellen a battle-scarred sergeant had insisted he must speak with her, but if she were too tired, he could stay over and talk with her the following morning. Ellen did not wish to spend the night wondering what his message might be, and though she was quite exhausted, insisted that they meet at once. H.T. took Ellen into one of the offices and sent an usher to bring the sergeant back.

Not knowing what the man might have to say, H.T. did not leave, but stood to one side, leaving them to face each other across the desk. The sergeant didn't hesitate, and began to speak immediately as if he had just been waiting to deliver his message and could not wait another second. He told her he had been the last person to speak with Jeremy and he had a message for her he did not fully understand. He said they had been part of a mash unit that had been caught in a German offensive and he and Jeremy were waiting with a group of wounded for an ambulance to arrive and take them to the rear. The other men had all been evacuated and the medical personnel had gone with them. The ambulance had not arrived and Jeremy was sure something had happened to put it out of service. They were both sure there wasn't much time left. He said Jeremy told him he should try to make it back to the main forces and bring help. The sergeant said he informed Jeremy he was the only one still on his feet trained to fight and he needed to stay and protect his men. Jeremy then told him he was the only one likely to make it and ordered him to go for help. When he had gone no more than half a mile, he found the ambulance and both medics were dead. When he tried to start the ambulance, a sniper opened fire and he realized, in his haste, he had walked into a trap. He was hit in both legs and would have been killed if the allied counterattack had not rescued him. He had directed them to where they would find Jeremy and the others, but they arrived too late. They had already been overrun. There was only one man found alive, and Jeremy was covering him with his own body. The young man who had forced himself from his wheelchair to salute the portrait of Jeremy was the only survivor.

Ellen suddenly realized he had not given her the message from Jeremy and asked for it. He told her the message had been burned with his clothes when he was taken to the hospital. He then told her Jeremy had made him memorize the message in case he was captured and that he could recall it word for word. He also said she would need to understand its meaning.

As the man repeated the message, Ellen realized why he could not understand—it was a message from Jeremy to her alone, and only she would know its true meaning.

"Dearest Ellen, always remember I love you and God loves you. Finally I can tell you, Tom was right, for now I can love myself."

Ellen knew at once the Italian Alps had been Jeremy's Golgotha—he had shouldered his cross and given his life in service for his men. Jeremy had found the greater love and now he was finally able to forgive himself, just as God had already forgiven him.

The sergeant had suddenly started talking again. This time he was talking about himself. He said he felt Jeremy had sent him for help because he knew there was no hope if he remained with them. He told Ellen he had lived his life for himself alone and had never done anything for anyone else unless there was something for him in return. He said he could never understand Jeremy because he was always living for others, and he could never see what it was he hoped to get in return. He had expressed this to some of his men, but they had told him he would never understand until he knew the Christ Jeremy served. He then said, "I came bearing Jeremy's message, but I also came because I want to know this Christ whom Jeremy served. I want to know this Christ who can inspire a person to live for others, and die for others without fear."

Ellen asked H.T. to give the sergeant a room in the dormitory for the night and she would talk with Tall Tom Dawson the next morning and see if he could come up with a plan that might help. Tom was now running a house for street people in Atlanta and Ellen was meeting with him the following morning to determine how she could best help with his work. Tom was getting older, and too many nights in tent meetings were taking their toll. Wes was still with Tom, but Ellen knew that lack of help and money to finance the things they needed had made their progress very slow. Ellen had asked H.T. for help and planned to give as much financial help as she possibly could.

When Ellen met with Tom the following morning, he told her about his new work and how it was like finding a new life. He praised Wes and told Ellen how dedicated he had become to their work. Wes, it seemed, had been searching for something to give his life meaning. In service to these homeless people, he had found joy and contentment.

When Ellen asked Tom what he needed most, he quickly replied, "A truck." He explained at present when people donated things they needed, it was necessary to rent a truck for pickup. Tom went on to explain, "Owning our own truck would make it possible to cover the city on a regular schedule and it would also make it possible to call and ask people for the things they needed."

Ellen called H.T. and he told her a box van would be ready for Tom when he was ready to return to Atlanta. Ellen gave Tom a cash gift and the two of them went through Jeremy's things. It was a difficult task for them both, but they knew Jeremy would want his things to be used by people who needed them most.

Ellen then told Tom about Sergeant Paul Adams and his request that they help him find Jeremy's Christ. Tom was deeply moved, but expressed to Ellen his doubt that he might be able to lead this man to Christ if Jeremy had not succeeded. Then, on second thought, Tom expressed the feeling that Paul had already seen Christ in Jeremy's life—it was simply a matter of needing some guidance.

Ellen sent for Paul and he and Tom talked. After talking for a short time, Tom told Paul all he needed was to see Christ's workers in action and experience the joy that comes from service to others through love. Tom explained that once he experienced the joy of letting Christ's love flow through him to others, he would understand what Jeremy had lived and died for. Tom further explained to Paul the work they were doing and that many of the men they served were returned veterans who had not been able to come to grips with life since their return home. He told Paul he would be able to reach many where others had failed because he could understand their suffering.

Tom explained to Paul their biggest roadblock was a shortage of cash and that there were times he and Wes were not able to pay themselves anything for weeks. Paul told Tom he didn't need money because he had a limited disability pension—as long as he had a bed and food to eat, he had no problems. Paul also explained he was not able to do heavy lifting because of his wounds, but he could drive a truck and do light housework. Tom and Paul left the following morning for Atlanta, with Paul driving a new box van donated by H.T. As she watched them leave, Ellen marveled at what God could do with a man like Tom, who lived by the motto, "Do what you can with what you have, where you happen to be."

Chapter XXIV

It was about a month later that Ellen received a letter from the War Department informing her that many of the men who had fallen could be returned home and that Jeremy was one of those. If Ellen wished Jeremy's body returned home, it would be necessary for her to file the enclosed papers. It was also requested that she let her wishes be known either way. Ellen spent hours that night trying to make a decision. She went to sleep with the matter still unresolved.

As Ellen slept, the problem unresolved, she started to dream she saw Jeremy and he was preaching. Jeremy's voice had that calming effect on her as it always had when he preached. It was the kind of dream one enjoys and feels totally comfortable with. Then suddenly Ellen recognized the sermon, and it shocked her fully awake. The sermon was one Jeremy had preached when trying to ease the minds of people who had loved ones listed as missing in action. Knowing these people were troubled not knowing where their loved ones were, Jeremy had touched on a point that had never left her mind. Jeremy had said, "The spirit of the dead shall come forth from the steaming jungles; they shall be raised from the depths of the seas; their spirits shall escape the burning tanks and planes; each shall be greeted by the Holy Spirit and each one received at a special place in the kingdom of God. They shall forever dwell in a heavenly place, for they have already experienced hell for the sake of others." Ellen had found her answer. She knew that Jeremy would prefer his body remain buried alongside those he had loved and served. Ellen completed the form instructing those concerned what they should do. Then almost without thought, Ellen wrote in the space reserved for comments, "HE IS RISEN."

Ellen, reading over the form and realizing what she had written, remembered the words Jeremy had once spoken to her, "You are a Christian, you just don't know it yet." In that moment, Ellen knew she had become a follower of Christ. She went to bed and slept a peaceful sleep. When Ellen awoke the next morning, she found a new joy in just living. She knew she had not changed from the person she was the previous day, but now, past sins were forgiven, and she had a new source of strength and power that would enable her to face the future. This was what Jeremy had left her and it would bring new purpose to her life as she shared with others.

Chapter XXV

The next few months were busy ones as Ellen assumed additional duties in the school's operation. H.T. never seemed to rest and, at times, Ellen wondered where he got all the drive. Then she realized it was the same thing that drove Jeremy. It was the knowledge that so many things needed to be done and there was no assurance there would be time enough to do them. Ellen kept in touch with Tom and was pleased to hear that Wes and Paul were working out so well. Tom had great praise for both of his helpers and was making big plans to serve the thousands who would be coming home now that the war had ended in Europe. On May 7, 1945, the war ended in Europe and all across America, people celebrated, but there were many like Ellen who could not join in the festivities. Their pain was too great.

The most enjoyable times for Ellen were when she could visit Dot or Dot was able to come visit her. When H.T. and Con were traveling, Dot always came to visit, and these were special times because they were free to do anything they wished, not that either of the men would object to them spending time together. It just seemed there was always so much work to be done.

With all the activity going on around her, Ellen had lost track of time, and was completely taken by surprise when she checked her calendar and saw the time had arrived to decide on a new president for the school. Ellen knew that several men had been interviewed for the position, and it was simply a matter of the board coming to a decision. Ellen was not concerned, because she had saved enough money to get her own place to live and to also go to school and decide what she wished to do in the future.

Before Ellen could leave for the office the following morning, H.T. called and said he would like to drop by for coffee. This had been his procedure when Jeremy was living, but he had always met her at the office and never came by the house unless Dot and Con were there. When H.T. came through the door, Ellen knew immediately that he was struggling with a problem that had him quite upset, and this was unusual for him. Ellen had never known H.T. to let any emotion interfere with his coming to a rational decision, and many people felt this had a lot to do with his success. Thinking he was concerned because the time had come for him to tell her she must move, Ellen began the conversation by trying to reassure him that everything was fine with her and she was not worried about her future.

H.T. quickly assured Ellen that this was not the problem he was struggling with because everything for her welfare had been carefully worked out. If she were willing, he had any number of opportunities for her working in his organization. She could pick where she wished to work—there were opportunities everywhere. She could even move closer to Dot if she wished. She would be paid sixty thousand dollars a year to start, and there was always plenty of room for advancement.

H.T. then began telling Ellen what was really troubling him, and he started by telling her how much he had always loved Jeremy, Dot, and Con. H.T. said he had always loved the three of them as he loved his two daughters and he had hoped when they first met he would eventually feel the same about her. This had been a problem for him because the opposite was true, and for many years he had loved her as a woman. This love had left him with a great burden of guilt as long as Jeremy lived.

H.T. went on to explain to Ellen that aside from his great love for Jeremy, his loving her was also a reason he worked so hard to keep Jeremy from going into combat. "Ellen, my feelings for you are so strong I have never trusted myself to be alone with you. I tell you this now fearing I may jeopardize our friendship, but I can no longer live with this secret I am so burdened with. You married before as a matter of necessity and that is the reason I am opening other opportunities for you to make your own decision. I could never bear to think you had married me for security, so your future is secure whatever your choice. Ellen, I love you and want you to be my wife. Think this through carefully, because I am twice your age, but it would mean everything to me having you share the remaining years of my life. Knowing I will, in all probability, die before you, I would have you share equally with my daughters in my estate. This is not an effort to buy your love, but what is necessary for me to do so that you will not be left without resources."

Ellen thought this must be the longest proposal on record. Ellen asked for time to think and invited H.T. for breakfast the following morning and promised she would give her answer then. Knowing his anxiety, Ellen embraced him and doing so realized she had never before so much as touched his hand.

H.T. left immediately and Ellen was glad he did, for she knew the feelings she was having had to show in her face. Ellen had not expected to feel this way, but knew after thinking about it, it was to be expected, for it had been nearly two years since a man held her in his arms. Ellen decided she would wait until she could think more clearly and be sure her decision was the right one. Ellen went for a walk around campus, but tried not to think about her decision. Finally, Ellen decided she needed to be occupied, and going to her office, worked at every disagreeable task she had left undone, keeping herself too busy to think.

The following morning if H.T. wanted reassurance, it was that kind of day: sunny, mild, and perfect for golf, a picnic, or even the answer to a marriage proposal. Ellen opened the door as H.T. came up the steps and they went into the library closing the door behind them. Ellen had left instructions with her servants to have breakfast ready in thirty minutes. Ellen did not hesitate, but moved immediately into the business at hand. "I will not tell you that I love you, H.T., and you know that I married twice before for reasons other than love. I was fortunate enough to find love in my marriage to Jeremy, and if we are married, it will always be my prayer that love will follow. I say if because before we can marry, you must agree to a premarital contract." H.T. looked stunned, so Ellen rushed ahead with her demands. "I have talked with Con and he tells me I am entitled to share equally in your estate with your two daughters, but I do not want this. Knowing them, they would not resent it, but I could never bear having other people say I married you for your money. It is my wish to be excluded from this, and Con has told me I can refuse and he can legally put it in writing. I feel as you do, that I need some kind of security, so I have one request. You have offered me five thousand dollars per month if I will work for you, and as your wife, I want to work with you. My request is that five thousand dollars be invested for me each month and that you instruct me so that sometime in the future I will be able to make those investments myself. This does not need to be in writing because it concerns only us. I trust you completely. If it were not so, I would not marry you."

H.T. was surprised and it took him several seconds to answer her, but years later she would remember his words. "Ellen, you are giving up a lot for a little, but you will never regret it." H.T. took her in his arms and held her gently. She raised her face and their lips met in a lingering kiss that revealed a passion long suppressed. H.T. and Ellen had only a few minutes to talk and make plans before going in to breakfast, but they were in full agreement on one point—the marriage would take place as soon as possible. They had their breakfast in an atmosphere of quiet assurance that can only come when two people have come to a decision they feel is good, and both have made it without reservations.

Chapter XXVI

The next week, Ellen moved out of the president's house and the newly installed president and his family moved in. H.T. planned to spend the next month helping the new man get a grip on things because he had decided it was time for him to give up his active role in the school's operation and to serve only on the board of trustees.

They talked with Dot and Con and it was decided that Ellen would live with them until the wedding. This would give Dot an opportunity to help Ellen find a suitable place for them to live. Dot knew the kind of accommodation needed because she was familiar with the lavish entertaining necessary to keep H.T. in touch with all of his extensive business empire. Ellen found several places she considered adequate, but each time Dot told her they were just too small to meet their needs. Finally, they found a large place ten miles from where Dot and Con lived. There were ten acres of land, a guest house, and servants' quarters.

Ellen liked the house but could not imagine ever needing such grand accommodations. H.T. was pleased and told Ellen to remodel the house the way she wanted it. He secured an architect and turned over to him the job of building a swimming pool, bath house, and tennis courts. All this was accomplished in less than two months and they were married in a small quiet ceremony in Dot's parlor.

H.T. left everything for Con to handle and they left for Europe on their honeymoon. They took their private railcar to New York, and Ellen was reminded again of that first honeymoon. She also wondered if H.T. had heard how just the sound of a train would turn her on and had picked that mode of transportation for that reason. Before they reached New York, Ellen also wondered if she was easy to please or just lucky in her choice of men. She had heard that men slow down sexually when they get older but, after being with H.T., she was convinced they had to be much older than sixty. Jane had also been right, "Sex couldn't make a marriage, but it could certainly unmake one." When Ellen thought of sex, she always remembered the motherly-looking middle-aged woman at one of the parties they had attended. She had had a few too many drinks and when someone mentioned sex, remarked, "The worst I ever had was wonderful."

Ellen and H.T. booked passage on the most deluxe ocean liner available out of New York. Ellen had never been on a ship before and found it to be the most relaxing and enjoyable travel she had ever experienced. They spent hours on deck and Ellen never tired of watching the wide expanse of water as far as her eyes could see. For the first time, Ellen could understand how men could be drawn to the seas, and could spend most of their life there.

They landed in England and the sights that greeted them took their breath away. It had been almost two years since the war had ended, but the devastation caused by German bombs and rockets was still very evident. H.T. told Ellen he was sure it would take at least five more years to complete the rebuilding.

They flew from London to Paris and Ellen found that flying was a great way to get somewhere in a hurry, but not nearly as enjoyable as travel by train or ship. Ellen found flying so boring she never traveled that way again, if some other means were available.

They were the perfect tourists. H.T. had been to the continent many times and was able to show Ellen all the worthwhile places without the services of a guide. The sights H.T. was familiar with took on new meaning for him because of the joy they brought to Ellen.

They had shopped for antiques and artwork in London, but the things available in Paris were unbelievable. There were small shops everywhere and people who needed money to rebuild and get on with their lives were selling collections of art and antiques in large quantities. Ellen cautioned H.T. that they did not know the exact measurements of the rooms in their new house and that many of the things they were buying might not fit. H.T. told her not to worry, that anything they bought and could not use would bring a good profit at home.

They left Paris and went by train to Berlin. Ellen had thought the destruction could not be worse than in London and was shocked to see the ruins that allied bombing had caused in Berlin. Ellen would learn later that there was not a corner of Germany that had been spared. The allies had made sure that every German would know the horror of modern warfare. They found that many Germans had found a way to preserve the valuable furniture and art objects and were eager to sell. They continued to buy and Ellen found that H.T. was skilled at recognizing the real and the fake in both furniture and in art. Ellen loved the porcelain and the old clocks they found in Germany, but the most valuable thing she got on the trip was an education in buying she received as she watched H.T.

After a week in Berlin, they decided they would fly to Rome rather than travel by rail. Because of the extensive damage done to the rail system by allied bombing, the train schedule could not always be relied on. Most of their purchases in Rome were art, and Ellen left these purchases to H.T. because all she had learned about art at this time was the fact that it cost enormous amounts of money. H.T. showed Ellen the most important sights in Rome, but again the destruction around them made it hard to appreciate the ancient treasures left by past generations. As Ellen looked at all the things around her that had been destroyed, she wondered how the people kept from being in a constant state of depression. To Ellen, they were a grim reminder of death and sorrow.

Chapter XXVII

After about a week in Rome, H.T. told Ellen he had an appointment at the embassy that afternoon. This was not unusual because he had visited the embassy in both London and Paris. His business contacts were worldwide and this made it necessary for him to know the people of the diplomatic corps on a personal basis. As she always did, Ellen spent part of the afternoon in the hotel beauty salon and the rest writing letters.

H.T. arrived back at about four thirty in the afternoon and was carrying a packet of paper to show Ellen. H.T. told Ellen he had gone to the embassy to find out how he could locate where Jeremy was buried and the best way to go about visiting his grave. He also told Ellen it was not necessary for her to go if she didn't wish to. He had not told her earlier because he was not sure it could be arranged, and he didn't want to disappoint her. Ellen did wish to go but had not mentioned it earlier because she was not sure how he would feel about it with them on their honeymoon. H.T. opened his package and spread the maps on the bed so they might study them.

They decided they would travel by car and by train. The final part of their journey would be through the Poe Valley on the Brenner Pass line. H.T. not only had the maps and train schedules but a list of good places to stop overnight. They decided to eat an early evening meal, retire early, and then finalize their plans the following morning.

After an early breakfast the following morning, they went over their maps again and tried to make some kind of workable schedule, but found the train schedules were in such disarray it was almost impossible to make any definite travel plans. There were numerous detours that must be taken because of bombed-out bridges that had never been replaced.

110

They also discovered travel by car would be difficult because, just like the rail bridges, many bridges on the main roads had not been replaced, making it necessary to use secondary roads. They decided trying to travel by car would be too difficult and their best chance was to let the rail authorities take the responsibility of getting them to their destination.

Verona was their destination because it was here the rail lines converged and they would take the Brenner Pass line across the Alps and into Austria or France, depending on which line was open at the time. These indefinite travel plans seemed strange, but later after seeing the destruction of the Italian rail system caused by American bombs, they understood.

They were told to be patient and enjoy the scenery because they would see a lot of Italy before they reached Bologna where Jeremy was buried. Because of the many bridges damaged and some completely destroyed, as well as damage to other rail facilities, the people responsible would not even estimate how long it would be before things returned to normal. They were assured that, once they reached Verona, they would find the rail system fully operational. There was a reason for this. Verona was the hub for the rail lines feeding the Brenner Pass line, Italy's link to central Europe.

They started on their journey and Ellen got another look at a country ravaged by war. She had seen the cities, but here she was seeing the systematic bombing that had completely shut down Italy. The bombs had so completely destroyed the transportation system that Germany could not maintain forces in Italy. They pulled into train stations consisting of only burned out buildings and the passengers didn't leave the train unless it was their destination. When they could see the highways from the train, the same conditions existed. There were reminders everywhere of the awful conflict that had taken place. Every kind of vehicle she had ever seen and some she had never seen were everywhere, just pushed to one side until time permitted their removal. In many places, they could see cars still using the pontoon bridges to cross streams. Farmers plowed around tanks and vehicles that still littered their fields. Ellen did not see it happen, but was told it was not unusual for a farmer's plow to hit a shell that had not exploded and become another casualty of a war long ended.

There were some things they saw that would be remembered and told later at parties—the farmer using an old discarded jeep to pull his hay rake. There were also things that were amusing. One such story was the day Ellen saw what she thought was the base of a silo, but realized it wasn't when she saw spigots around the base. H.T. told her it was used for stamping out the grapes. The grapes were put in the concrete bowl-like structure and men wearing hip boots would stomp around in them and the juice would run out the spigots around the base. When Ellen saw a farmer walk through the barnyard and then proceed to stomp the grapes, she told H.T. it was time to give up wine. He laughed and told her that was where the French wine got its body. They both had red wine with their evening meal.

After considerable backtracking and detours, they eventually reached Bologna. They recognized at once that heavy fighting had taken place here. There were signs of both heavy bombing and intense shelling by artillery. Ellen could never tell for sure if bombs or artillery shells had done the damage, but was sure there had been plenty of both. To the people who had lost so much, it probably didn't matter how they had lost it. Ellen did notice the people were dismantling the brick bunkers the Germans had used for their antiaircraft guns and using the materials to rebuild.

It had taken three days because of delays and rerouting, but Ellen never tired of train travel, so she was not the least bit tired. H.T. had been able to get the best accommodations the rail line had to offer so it had been a most enjoyable trip. After bathing, they went down to the hotel dining room and Ellen was surprised to find a wide variety of good food available. H.T. told her he had never experienced a shortage of food anywhere for those who had the money to pay. He told Ellen it is the nature of man to keep the best for those who have the most. H.T. went on to say it is only one more problem the world will have to solve if the world is ever to know peace.

It was still early when they finished eating and H.T. called the embassy to get directions so they might visit Jeremy's grave the following morning. H.T. was told he was expected and a driver would pick them up the following morning and drive them to Jeremy's grave site. The driver would also be at their disposal for the rest of the day. He would drive them where they wished to go and if they had no plans, would act as their guide. Ellen appreciated all her government wanted to do for her, but could not help wondering if everyone who had lost a loved one would receive such royal treatment.

Ellen knew the treatment she and H.T. were receiving was not typical, but was reserved for very important people such as her husband. Ellen knew this was not right, but also knew it was the way of the world and there wasn't anything she could do about it. The words of Tall Tom then came to mind, "Do what you can with what you have, where you happen to be." Ellen knew this was the answer, and was confident that one day she would be able to do more to right the wrongs of the world, and she made herself a promise that she would not forget. Ellen had been one of the have-nots of the world most of her life and it would be unthinkable for her to ever forget.

A car from the embassy picked them up the following morning and a young soldier acted as their chauffeur and guide. He reminded Ellen of the young men who had attended Jeremy's memorial service, and she wondered how much of this destruction he had seen happen. H.T. told her he had probably arrived here after most of the conflict had ended, otherwise he would have already rotated back to the states.

It was less than a thirty-minute drive from the hotel to the cemetery. They were expected because the iron gates were immediately opened and the guard gave the driver a map directing him to the grave site. There was acre after acre of white crosses.

To Ellen, it seemed impossible to find anything, but their driver must have been very familiar with his surroundings and was able to drive them directly to the grave site. As they walked to the grave, Ellen wondered how much their driver knew, and did it seem strange to him that a couple on their honeymoon would visit the grave of the bride's former husband? She knew he would have been even more confused if he had walked with them to the grave and seen the tears stream down H.T.'s face and seen the suffering there. Ellen had never doubted H.T. when he said he loved Jeremy as a son, but as she witnessed his grief, for the first time she realized the depth of that love. Ellen knew as they walked back to the car they could be mistaken by a stranger as father and daughter grieving over the loss of a son and brother. This thought had never entered Ellen's mind before, and it did not bother her now. If such a thought had ever occurred to H.T., he had never mentioned it to anyone. As they drew near one another now, it was as husband and wife consoling each other in the loss of someone they both held dear.

They thanked the young driver and told him once he had taken them back to the hotel the rest of the day was his because they were going to leave as soon as possible.

Their thinking was the same—they would feel better once they had left Bologna. They had visited the place where Jeremy had been laid to rest, but in their hearts they knew his spirit would be nearer them once they were back home and active once more in the school he had created.

Chapter XXVIII

They had no trouble making their arrangements to leave Italy, for they would find from this point on the repairs and rebuilding had been almost completed. They were routed from Bologna to Mantua and from there to Verona, the junction with the Brenner Pass line that would carry them out of Italy and into Central Europe. From this point on, the reconstruction had been expedited because the rail line was the main link between Italy and the rest of Europe.

They had not traveled far before they could see how difficult the rebuilding of the Brenner Pass line had been. The medium bombers, mainly the B-26s from Corsica, had bombed every bridge and marshalling yard to dust in their effort to keep the German Army from escaping out of Italy to join their comrades in one last-ditch effort to save their homeland. On the stretch of tract between Mantua and Verona there was one five-span bridge that had been completely rebuilt. The tracks had been moved some fifty yards to the right and a completely new bridge built, leaving the rubble of the old bridge in place.

After they left Verona, there was no more switching or going around by different routes—there was only one route as they climbed higher and higher into the Italian Alps. Ellen knew very little about geography, but she did remember the names of a few places: Rovereto, Trento, and high in the mountains a place called Bolzano. She remembered because those places had been so heavily bombed. An American soldier told them Bolzano had been hit especially hard because it was so close to the pass. The same soldier also gave them a history lesson, telling them the first road through the pass was built by the Roman legions. These cities were very familiar with war because the

Romans had passed through here as they made their conquests into central Europe. He added, "This time was different because never before in history has there been destruction equaling that done by the American Air Force."

The most beautiful part of the trip for Ellen was when the tracks skirted the shores of Lake Garda. H.T. told her it was the largest lake in Italy. On the mountains overlooking Lake Garda, Ellen could see many beautiful villas, and on the mountain peaks there was snow. This scene brought tears to her eyes, because Ellen remembered Jeremy had written how beautiful the mountains were.

Ellen remembered how Jeremy had written he hoped some day to spend a second honeymoon with her in one of these beautiful villas and hold her in his arms, before an open fire. Ellen felt like screaming as she thought of all the other men who had dreamed this same dream and never lived to bring it about. Ellen prayed those other women had found another man to love them as H.T. loved her. She was certain Jeremy had never made it this far up the Poe Valley but had only seen these beautiful mountains from a distance. Here, like everywhere, the bridges had been destroyed and had to be rebuilt. One conductor native to the area even pointed out to them places where the bombs had blasted the tracks off the side of the mountains. He told them many fliers died in these mountains, but many more infantry would have died if the Germans had been able to join forces with their troops in France and Austria.

Ellen was shocked as she saw the antiaircraft guns sticking out of the water in Lake Garda and could only imagine how deadly they must have been. She found herself hoping the barges had been sunk before the guns claimed too many lives. When Ellen realized what her thought had been, she shook in an effort to control her emotions, because she knew even one life was too many if the one who was lost had been yours.

Ellen didn't need to be reminded of the folly of war, but she was at a loss to explain the strange feeling that engulfed her when in an area where she knew many men had died. The same feeling came over her years later when she visited the battlefield at Gettysburg. To Ellen, it seemed the silence of death was straining to be heard.

It was night, and Ellen was sleeping when they went through the pass and down the French side of the Alps. She never knew what route they took as they made their way to Paris. The death and destruction of war had worn her out, and she was ready to go home.

From France, they took a boat across the channel to England, and then took the first available ship for home. The ocean voyage was a welcome time of rest and relaxation, but the motion of the ship never added to the thrill of sex like the sound of the rails or the blast of a train whistle. Ellen knew nothing could ever take the place of travel by train and was thankful they had their own private car waiting.

After docking in New York, they had their luggage taken directly to their railcar and were scheduled to leave the following morning. H.T. felt it would be better for them to stay the night in a hotel where they could have their evening meal and breakfast the following morning.

Because they were gone so long, Rufus had not made the trip with them, so it was necessary that they take their meals in the dining car. Ellen would always remember the shock that first day when she looked out the window of the dining car and saw no sign of mass destruction like she had become used to in Europe. It was like coming from another world or even another planet. The roads and bridges were all intact and the buildings had not been bombed into a charred mass. It was hard for Ellen to become accustomed to things normal again and she wondered how the people of the USA would react if they were ever called on to endure the real hardships of war.

They enjoyed the privacy of their own car again, and the knowledge that they would not be subject to delays or rerouting. They were met by Dot and Con and spent the night with them because they were sure things would not be in order at their new home. Ellen experienced a new joy, because it was the first time she could remember coming home to a family. Con and Dot had become her family and it gave her life new meaning.

When they arrived at their home the next morning, Ellen was amazed to see the large number of shipping crates filling one of the largest rooms in the house. H.T. had sent word they were not to be unpacked until he returned home. H.T. obtained men who were qualified to uncrate the expensive antiques, but he did not permit them to uncrate the expensive paintings unless he was present. For one whole week, Dot and Ellen watched as the men uncrated what they had bought, and tried to find a place for everything. It was just as Ellen feared. They had bought much more than they could use, and some things were just not suitable. The workers repacked the things that could not be used, and they were shipped to a famous auction house to be sold. Only then did Ellen realize what H.T. had meant when he said we will make a profit on what can't be used. She learned this was just another part of his business, the importing and selling of expensive antiques.

Once all of the unpacking was done and the furniture was in place, things were left to the interior decorators. They brought everything to Ellen for approval, so she and Dot had a lot of decision making to do for the next month. They only saw H.T. and Con for meals and at bedtime, because they were busy also, trying to catch up on all the work not attended to while H.T. was on their honeymoon. Most of every day was spent in the office complex that was part of Dot and Con's home. There was a constant stream of people from all over the world meeting for hours with H.T. and Con.

Ellen had never realized the amount of work that went into the running of such a large financial empire. A week seldom went by without a large dinner party to entertain clients and their families. H.T. had so many of his own people coming and going, as well as the leaders of every conceivable type of financial undertaking that Ellen saw why Dot chose such a large estate for them and why H.T. felt the need for such a large staff. Entertaining was a full-time job and Ellen loved it, but knew without Dot she could never handle everything.

Chapter XXIX

After Ellen had been home for a month, Dot handed her a check one morning for five thousand dollars saying, "This is your paycheck. I write everybody's check because when it is left to Con, he always forgets." Ellen, thinking it was the agreed-on money that H.T. was to invest for her, took it to him, but he said it was her pay because she and Dot were in charge of company entertainment. They had been too busy to think about her investments and had been married now for two months, so Ellen got her first lesson in investing with ten thousand dollars. H.T. also instructed her never to spend any of her salary for clothes or things needed at the house because these things would be paid for by him, and her salary was her spending money.

One night, as Ellen got ready for bed, she saw a box lying on her pillow and was shocked as she realized she had forgotten her first anniversary. Things had moved so fast, and life had been so full, she found it hard to believe a whole year had passed. The box contained a platinum tennis bracelet covered with diamonds, and even though she knew very little about jewelry, Ellen was sure it had cost more than the Mercedes she was driving. Ellen tried to apologize but H.T. said it just meant she wasn't bored and that was all he needed to know, and besides, as long as she was with him, there wasn't anything else in this world he needed to make him happy.

H.T. surprised them all one morning by announcing it was time to make a trip to promote the school and they would make plans to leave in the next four weeks. Their itinerary would coincide with the annual church meetings. The work Jeremy had done was having great results, and they must make sure the lines of communication between the school and the churches didn't break down. H.T. announced that Dr. Bradley White would be accompanying them on this trip. He wished to introduce Dr. White to the ministers and give him the opportunity to let them know about the counseling course available to them by correspondence and also in yearly seminars.

H.T. hadn't forgotten that Jeremy had said a great need would have to be met when the men came home from the war. It had been Jeremy's plan to graduate ministers trained in counseling to meet this need. H.T. had considered Dr. White the best man available to carry out Jeremy's wishes, and the course had been great training for the new ministers. They were ready now to make the course available as a part of the ongoing education for the older ministers.

Ellen learned that Dr. White had done extensive work with the Veterans Administration since the war, and H.T. felt he was the best qualified in the country. Ellen asked H.T. how Dr. White could take time to establish the course for the school, spend the time traveling to promote the program, and still keep his job with the Veterans Administration. H.T. told her all the work Dr. White did was free gratis, his family was wealthy, and he didn't need money.

She wondered what kind of person he would be because she had never met anyone who had everything he needed and could give time and energy only to those things he wished to do. As Ellen pondered this thought, she started thinking of all the things she might give her time and energy to if she were wealthy. She dismissed that thought as time wasted in daydreaming.

Ellen expected to meet someone entirely different from the person she met. Brad White was only a few years older than Ellen and very easy to talk with. He was everything except the distant introvert Ellen had expected him to be. They became friends instantly and became very good friends in the next two months.

Brad, Con, and Dot had their sleeping quarters in one car and H.T. and Ellen had theirs in the other car. They had the same three servants as the last trip, and this meant things ran smoothly. The workload for Con and H.T. was considerably lighter than before so this made for a more leisurely trip.

Dr. White was a great success in his work with the pastors, and his good looks were helpful in obtaining the support of their wives. H.T. made sure plans were made to accommodate the wives of ministers who registered for special sessions, leaving every stop with large groups pre-registered. Ellen was pleased with the results because she knew this project was first priority with Jeremy had he lived.

At many of the stops, H.T. and Con had business and legal problems they needed to take care of for some of the local churches. Oftentimes Dot went along to act as secretary. This left Ellen and Brad alone for long periods of time. Ellen told him more about her past life than anyone she had met since leaving Wes and Little Cosby behind. Brad listened to her life story and did so without criticism. This understanding of her past life made for a strong bond between them.

In their early conversation, Ellen questioned Brad about the need of the returning veterans. She knew Jeremy had said they needed psychological counseling, and asked Brad if they really needed psychiatric help. Brad assured her that Jeremy had been right, for his hardest job in the last two years had been convincing the Veterans Administration that these men didn't have a mental problem but simply had endured things that had a great impact on their lives and needed to talk to trained people who could make it possible for them to live with what they had been exposed to. Brad said he knew many of the returning veterans would never come to terms with this part of their lives until they had psychological counseling. Like Jeremy, he felt a trained group of ministers would be able to help many who otherwise would never receive help. Brad told Ellen the Veterans Administration now had a program under way to meet the needs and he was only on staff as a consultant.

Though Con didn't make friends easily, he seemed to get along well with Brad. Dot was hopeful he might sometime in the future be able to fill the void in Con's life left by Jeremy's death.

H.T. and Ellen had time to spend with each other because being in their own car ensured their privacy. Ellen knew she would cherish those two months for the rest of her life because she knew how much they had meant to H.T. H.T. seemed to cling to each moment they had together, being like a second honeymoon. As Ellen looked back on that time, she wondered if H.T. hadn't known deep inside this would be their last rail trip together. Ellen did know she had made a special effort to make it a memorable trip and was sure she had succeeded.

Chapter XXX

During one of Ellen's long talks with Brad, when H.T., Con, and Dot were not present, she jokingly told him, "I have revealed so much of my life to you that you have become my own personal shrink." Brad replied, "Ellen, I could never be your shrink. My feelings for you would never allow me to be objective." Ellen did not answer. If she felt there might be feelings other than a special friendship, there was never anything else that would indicate this to be true. Brad did learn all about her past because with him she was able to relate her past without reservations.

Through 1948 and 1949, H.T. and Brad worked very closely, not only in business affairs, but also in their extensive charity work. Quite often when they traveled, meetings kept H.T. occupied for long periods of time. This left Ellen and Brad on their own and they spent many enjoyable hours together. Ellen continued jokingly referring to Brad as her shrink. H.T. found this quite amusing, because Brad was a very serious person, and not many people took the liberty of teasing him.

It was on one of their business trips that H.T. suffered his first heart attack. H.T. and Ellen were alone at the time because Brad was giving a lecture at a medical meeting. Brad had just finished speaking when a portable phone was brought to him at the head table. It was Ellen calling from a nearby hospital and Brad left immediately. H.T. was feeling fine when Brad arrived at the hospital because the attack had been mild and the pain had already subsided. H.T. was insisting that he be allowed to leave, and the doctors, not wanting to take any chances with a person of his importance, were trying their best to get him to stay and let them monitor him through the night. H.T. had made up his mind, and not even Brad could change it. Only after Ellen took charge and ordered that a bed be brought into the room so she could spend the night with H.T. did he consent to stay.

Brad took care of getting all of their things back to the railcar and they went directly home, canceling the rest of their engagements. On their arrival home, H.T. was examined by his own doctors and was ordered to slow down, especially where travel was involved. This changed their lifestyle some, but not much. They walked more just as the doctors ordered, which gave them more time together. They also spent more time with Dot and Con because not traveling made it necessary for H.T. to communicate with his managers through Con's office.

The biggest change was in the time they spent together going over Ellen's investments. She had been active in investing her five thousand dollars each month for some time, but now H.T. was insisting that she review her investments each day and make decisions on when to buy and sell her stocks.

The other more drastic change was in their sex life. Ellen was sure he had become much more active since he had more leisure time and they could spend more time together. Ellen was perfectly willing, but she was so concerned about his health, she could no longer enjoy their lovemaking. This had never happened to Ellen before and it was a matter of great concern.

On Ellen's day to go to the beauty parlor, she told H.T. she would be a little late because she needed to do some shopping. She went by his doctor's office without calling because she had to make sure H.T. did not learn of her visit. Ellen was not comfortable discussing her concern with the doctor, but knowing it must be done, approached the subject head on. The doctor's advice was do not hesitate to do whatever H.T. wishes to do, because sexual activity isn't likely to bother his heart. In fact, the doctor said the worry and anxiety he might feel if he thought he could not live an active life, potentially could do much more harm. This made the time they could now spend together, with H.T. relaxed and unhurried, the most treasured of Ellen's memories. She once jokingly told Dot, "I think I know now what people mean by quality time." Ellen became more aware of how much time Con worked and thought how much it would mean to Dot if he could give her more of his time, but she was not sure Con would be able to relax away from his work.

They did not entertain as much as they had in the past, but it was still necessary to bring in the key people in the organization for business meetings. Dot and Ellen continued to organize the business parties, but Ellen left most of the work to Dot and only helped when H.T. was working with Con.

Ellen noticed that H.T. was making a special effort to have her meet the key people in the organization and was making sure she understood the duties of each one. She was not sure what this meant and finally asked Dot if she could shed some light on what H.T. was trying to do. Dot said he was simply trying to make sure she would be able to take care of things if it ever became necessary. She warned Ellen not to tell H.T. what she had told her. Dot also told her not to worry about things because Con would always be available to help her. Dot also instructed Ellen to try and absorb all she could that H.T. was trying to teach her because he was the one with the golden touch.

What Dot had said worried Ellen, but she had always lived a life of uncertainty and had come to make the most of each day, confident she could cope with whatever tomorrow might bring.

It was an evening after one of their large business meetings that H.T. had his final heart attack. Dot, Con, and Brad were spending the night and they had gone into the study to finalize their plans for a large charity ball to be held the following week. Ellen and H.T. were sitting on the couch when he suddenly clutched his chest. Brad was immediately by his side and stretched him out with his head resting in Ellen's lap. Con called an ambulance while Dot and Brad worked to make H.T. comfortable. H.T. was not excited and didn't seem to be serious after the first pains subsided. He simply talked quietly with Ellen while they waited for the ambulance to arrive. The things H.T. was telling her did not seem unusual to Ellen. He was just telling her some everyday things she needed to check on and telling her again that Con had knowledge of any details she might need. When the ambulance arrived, Ellen told Dot to get her coat and prepared to go with H.T. in the ambulance. H.T. objected, telling her riding in the ambulance was too dangerous and he would rather she follow with the others in the car. Not wanting to worry him, Ellen kissed him good-bye and H.T. smiled at her as they placed him in the ambulance.

Ellen rode with the others in the car and fully expected to find H.T. much better when she reached the hospital. She was sure H.T. would be giving everyone a hard time and demanding that he be allowed to go home. This was not the case. The young doctor who attended H.T. in the ambulance informed them H.T. had suffered a massive heart attack before they reached the hospital and had died instantly. Ellen was sure he knew he would not make it and had kept her out of the ambulance to spare her. They had enjoyed five years of married life and H.T. had died just a few days after their fifth wedding anniversary and his sixty-fifth birthday.

Chapter XXXI

When they reached home, Dot told Ellen everything was under control because Con had been given his instructions in detail by H.T. several months ago. Brad encouraged her to rest and wait until the following morning before trying to absorb any details or make any plans. Ellen agreed but insisted there were some things she must go over with them at once. She informed them a memorial service must be arranged at the college because this was what H.T. had requested. Ellen also informed them he would then be transported to her hometown and be buried in her family plot where she would one day be buried between him and her father. Ellen told them this was not her plan but was what H.T. had asked her to do. Dot immediately objected.

Dot reminded Ellen she was only thirty-five and would certainly be married again, and possibly have children, who might not understand if Ellen were not buried next to their father. She also tried to convince Ellen the man she married might also frown on such an arrangement. Ellen had some misgivings herself and turned to Brad for advice.

Brad had an immediate answer—it seemed he was expecting such a question to arise and had thought everything through. Brad had a feeling H.T. had a motive in wanting Ellen to return to the place of her birth and seeing once again where she had come from. He was sure H.T. wanted one day to have Ellen laid to rest next to him, but he also knew him too well to think he wanted Ellen to endure the pain that would come from facing her past just so he could have what he wanted. He told them he and H.T. had discussed the fact that Ellen was carrying around too much baggage from her past and needed to put these things behind her. Ellen was sure Brad's following remarks were those of the professional and were also probably slanted because of his confessed inability to always be objective where she was concerned.

Brad spoke his next words directly to Ellen, "You have always felt less of yourself than you should, because you feel you have used men. This is not the case, because you have given just as much, and on many occasions more than you have received from the men in your life. Your brother took your love and gave nothing in return and was finally responsible for your losing your father. Your father received your love and returned your love, but he loved your brother more. You still blame yourself because you married Wes as a convenience, but you gave more to him than he ever gave to you. Though you never came to love Wes, you did help him find a life he never knew existed for him. It is true you used Jeremy, but you must remember he also used you. Jeremy was your way out of an impossible situation, but you helped him to find the life he had lost and were really his salvation. The wonderful part of your relationship with Jeremy was the strong love that grew between you. You did not marry H.T. because you needed to, and you didn't marry him for money. You proved that in the beginning. I doubt even now you realize why you married H.T. He made millions and used what he made to make a difference, but he had never taken the time to enjoy just living for him. Those five years H.T. lived with you were his life. H.T. once told me, 'Ellen has lived her life for everyone else, and when I am gone, I want her to live Ellen's life.' H.T. is not asking that you do these things for him, Ellen, but rather that you do them for yourself so you can leave behind past hurts, old memories, and start a new life. Dot does have a point there are men you could marry who might not understand, but such a man you do not need, because it would mean he does not love you enough."

When Brad said those words, Ellen was looking at Dot, and a look came over Dot's face Ellen did not understand, but with all the other things on her mind, she didn't think to talk to Dot about it later. Dot then brought their meeting to a close by saying, "On second thought, I feel H.T. was right, you do need to go back and rid yourself of the excess baggage, so you can move on with your life."

Ellen decided she would wait until morning to make a decision and felt they should all retire so they would be fresh for the things they must face the following morning. Brad offered to give her something to help her sleep, but she refused, because she knew there were too many things she must think through. The first thing Ellen knew she must decide was what her life would be. For the first time, Ellen realized her life had never been planned. Everything she had ever done had been dictated by events and circumstances. She now had a big decision to make—just what kind of life did she want?

H.T. had said Ellen must live her life, and everyone else seemed to agree, but she found herself facing the question, what does Ellen want Ellen's life to be? Her first thought was family, and suddenly she realized her only family consisted of Con, Dot, and Brad. Ellen's next thought hit hard, because she thought of children, and suddenly reality kicked in. If she wanted children of her own, she needed to marry in the next three years.

Ellen had never looked at her life in this way before, probably because her previous marriages had not been conducive to a normal family life. There was no longer any doubt in her mind if it was to be Ellen's life it must include more than two people. Certain of what she wanted for her future, Ellen was finally able to relax and get a few hours of much needed sleep.

Ellen awoke early the next morning, and the thought of what she would do concerning where she would bury H.T. came to mind. She fully understood Dot's concern, but in the clear light of day, realized that Brad had been right. Any man who truly loved her would not be concerned with such a trivial matter. Going back home just now and facing all the memories was another matter. She did not want to face this because she knew all the heartaches and pain that made up her past would come flooding back.

Ellen did not want to face up to this, but she knew it was Brad's professional opinion that she must face her past and put it behind her if she wished to get on with her life. As so often happened when she was confronted by a difficult decision, Jeremy came to mind. She remembered how he spent hours in prayer working out problems. Her life with H.T. had been problem free, and her only concern in the last five years had been his happiness. Now she had to deal with a decision she did not wish to make, but one only she could make. After an hour of meditation and prayer, her thoughts returned to Jeremy and the explanation he once gave her about the story of Lot's wife. Ellen had told him she did not understand why God would turn Lot's wife into a pillar of salt just because she looked back toward Sodom and Gomorrah. Jeremy explained that God had spared Lot and his family because they were supposed to be committed to a new life and he had warned them not to look back. When Lot's wife looked back, it was an indication she was not fully committed to the new way of life, but still longed for the old life. Jeremy had explained the moral of the story is simple—if one is fully committed to a new way of life, one must leave all the old baggage behind and never look back. Ellen knew the influence of Jeremy in her life would always be with her. There was a spot in Ellen's heart that would always belong to Jeremy, and Ellen knew this was something else the man she married would need to understand, but as Brad had said, if the man she married loved her enough he would understand.

After the four of them had finished breakfast, Ellen asked that they join her in the study so she could tell them her plans. She explained to them that she had decided to carry out H.T.'s wishes. He would be laid to rest in her family plot where she at sometime in the future would be buried between him and her father. She emphasized that she agreed with Brad that she must do this in order to leave her past behind her. Ellen also told them after the final prayer, she would leave the cemetery immediately without speaking to anyone and they might not see her for several months. Ellen promised she would contact Dot and let her know how she was doing, but she felt it was necessary to be alone so she could think clearly and make her plans for the future.

Ellen knew the investments she and H.T. had made for her were now near the million-dollar mark, but she needed to know from Con if there was immediate cash available to her. Con then informed her that a million-dollar life-insurance policy would provide all the cash she would need until a minimum amount of paperwork could be filed. Con told Ellen he should let her know as near as possible the full extent of her financial holdings. He told her when she refused one-third share of H.T.'s wealth, as was her due under the law, but instead asked only that he invest five thousand dollars for her each month, while teaching her to invest, he had done as she wished and then set things in motion the way he wanted them to be. The day before they were married, he had put his entire holdings in trust for his two daughters. This trust was handled by Con and 25 percent was his personally, regardless of how large it might become. This agreement had been entered into when he gave up his practice of law and became financial manager of H.T.'s financial empire. The daughters were free to buy him out at any time, but this was not likely until their sons became old enough for him to train them to take over. This was what Dot had meant when she said they had no financial worries. This was H.T.'s way of doing business. He wanted the person who looked after his wealth to have a personal stake in what he was able to achieve. Con then proceeded to give Ellen additional information that only he and Dot knew. After putting everything in trust for his daughters, H.T. had started over. This new company was jointly owned by H.T. and Ellen. Also, things were owned under a right of survivorship, and now Ellen was owner of everything, as soon as a limited number of papers were filed. Con also let Ellen know he owned 25 percent of this company, as well as the company he watched after for the daughters. Ellen was finding it hard to grasp, when Con told her she was now a millionaire many times over. She could only remember Dot's words, "H.T. is the man with the golden touch." She also remembered the words of H.T. when she refused a portion of his wealth and instead asked only that he make investments for her. His words had been, "You have refused a lot and asked for a little, but you will never regret it."

Ellen asked Con if she were gone for as much as six months, were there any papers she needed to sign for him to handle everything. He told her that authority was already his, but she had the power to revoke it at any time, and that she was in a financial position to buy him out at any time. She assured Con that was the farthest thing from her mind, that running a financial empire was not part of her plans for the future. Her only request was that he try to get more help so he and Dot could have more time together. In a flash, Ellen remembered her thoughts when told Brad didn't have to work, but was wealthy enough to live his life as he chose. The same now applied to her. Ellen knew this new wealth could make her life more complicated, because it carried with it not only opportunity but also responsibility. Ellen hoped she could meet those responsibilities as well as Brad had in his life.

Knowing she might not have another opportunity to talk with each one privately before she left, Ellen embraced each of her friends and thanked them for all they had done for her. Con, still shy as ever, returned her embrace, but said nothing. Dot assured her they would watch after things and be there to welcome her home. Brad kissed her cheek and whispered, "I'll be waiting."

Dot assisted Ellen in making funeral arrangements for the following day, and Brad took care of scheduling. Because it was a three-hour drive to the grave site, Brad had made it very clear to everyone taking part that the service must be over by ten o'clock sharp. The car had picked them up at eight o'clock and they arrived early to assure the service would start on time. As they drove through the entrance and around the circle drive, Ellen received that warm feeling she always had when she saw the words "Major Jeremy Grimes Memorial Chapel." Today, that feeling took on even more meaning because now two men she had loved, and who had loved each other, were now joined in life eternal.

The only change in the chapel since Ellen's last visit was a plaque hanging next to Jeremy's portrait. The plaque stated that a portrait of H.T. Thompson had been commissioned by a well-known artist and would hang here when finished. In smaller print, it read, "Given in loving memory of a dear friend, Dr. Bradley White." The two daughters were there with their husbands and children and they greeted Ellen as they would have greeted another sister. Ellen had not realized it before, but this had always been the way she had been received by both girls. Probably they felt more comfortable with this type of relationship because they were all so near the same age.

The service did end at ten o'clock sharp and they had a leisurely drive to the grave site, arriving just five minutes before the service was to start.

Now after an hour, the service was about to end. Ellen wondered if they had used the same service as was used twenty years earlier when she had stood on this same spot, a fifteen-year-old girl crying for her father. Now, at age thirty-five, Ellen did not feel the same pain she felt then. She did not feel it was because she loved any less, but just that with maturity, death had become a part of life, and she had learned to accept it as such.

The real difference today had been the pain Ellen had felt as her life unfolded before her. Ellen wondered if the same would not have been true of anyone's life. It could not be possible that only her life had been so full of pain and sorrow. Ellen made God a promise that she would use her new wealth to relieve the burdens that so many carried. Ellen, sensing that the minister was about to finish with the closing prayer, looked once more toward Con, Dot, and Brad. She saw that Brad had not closed his eyes but was looking at her. The love Ellen saw in Brad's eyes brought the only joy Ellen's heart had felt that day.

Ellen heard the minister say, "Amen," and without hesitation, turned and walked away. Her car was parked where Brad said it would be, in front of the hearse, where she would not be blocked. She started her white Mercedes, put it in gear, drove to the nearest exit, and never looked back.

Chapter XXXII

Ellen was startled by the sound of a buzzer, but realized instantly what it was. Brad had told her she was low on gas because he could not fill her car. She had failed to give him the key to the gas cap. Ellen had been driving and thinking, finishing the plans she had made in the last thirty-six hours. Looking around her, Ellen saw she was only a short distance from Sevierville, so the low gas supply would not be a problem. She could fill the car with gas and also find something to eat. Thinking of food made her realize she had eaten very little in the last twenty-four hours. Ellen had not told anyone where she was going, but she had decided the night before she must return to the mountains.

Ellen had experienced the renewal of strength in Jeremy when he had returned to these hills and she was seeking that same renewal for herself. The people in her life that had meant the most, both living and dead, were a part of this rugged country, and she wanted to begin her new life in the place she felt God could best speak to her and give her guidance.

Ellen would have liked to talk with Mag, but Mag was no longer among the living. She had returned from whence she came, and a person's opinion as to where that might be depended on how each individual might have known her.

Polly had written Ellen a few months after Jeremy was killed and told her that Mag had died. "Mag's work is done and she has gone to be with Jeremy."

Ellen knew she could never contact the spiritual world that Mag seemed to move to and from, but she knew nevertheless that she could find Jeremy here in the place he loved. He seemed to guide her even now when she must make decisions, and knew when she and Lou knelt to pray, she would feel the touch of Jeremy's hand as she had years before.

Thinking of the time Lou and Jeremy had prayed for Jimmy as the three of them held hands, Ellen felt again the warm glow inside and felt again the nearness of Christ she had felt that day. Lou Walker, her son Jimmy, and her daughter Amy, widow of her brother Bruce, were her extended family and she must talk to Lou and make plans for the future.

Lou had written Ellen when Jimmy was wounded and sent home. It had been not more than one month after Jeremy was killed. "Jimmy has come home a different person," she wrote. "Guns make him physically sick. Jimmy was a dedicated hunter, but the first day back he saw the old hog rifle hanging over the mantle, went outside and vomited. I buried that old gun and also every piece of the old still. I have made sure those signs of violence will never make Jimmy ill again."

When Ellen received that letter from Lou, she realized Lou had buried the past and now looked only to the future. Ellen's next thought was how Jimmy had been wounded. The premature explosion of a grenade had cost Jimmy his right hand. It had been removed at the wrist. That hand had squeezed off the shots. Now it was buried in the jungles and was part of his past. Others might not know it, but Ellen knew there were things in Jimmy's mind that could never be buried. For that reason, Ellen was elated when she received Lou's next letter. She wrote that Jimmy has been reading a letter from Jeremy that he received after we prayed for him here in the mountains. Jimmy carried it with him all this time and seems to live by one small sentence. "Do what you can, with what you have, where you happen to be."

Jimmy has decided to go to East Tennessee State University under the new G.I. Bill. He wants to become a teacher. He talked with Polly, who for years dreamed of opening a school in conjunction with the orphanage that would be open to any child of the mountains who wishes to come. The plan was for Jimmy to come back and help Polly. It will need to start small because of limited finances, but they have both found confidence in the words: "Do what you can, with what you have, where you happen to be,"—the new school motto.

Shortly after receiving the letter from Lou, Ellen had received a letter from Polly. The spirit of her letter revealed to Ellen the happiness of a person who had received a new lease on life. "At my age," Polly wrote, "I know I can never live to see my dream fulfilled, but now I can see it started."

This had all begun about the time she and H.T. had married, so Ellen had been able to send some money to help make their project a reality.

Ellen had heard again from Polly when Jimmy had returned last year with a teaching certificate and a new bride. "Her name is Judy and she is what we needed," Polly wrote. "Most of all, though, she is what Jimmy needed. He is still prone to moments of deep sorrow and seems to be fighting a darkness deep within. At these times Judy is the calming ingredient that brings him back to reality and a renewed purpose of living. When I see this, the lines of an old hymn come to mind, 'There is a balm in Gilead to heal the sinsick soul.' I am also reminded of Mag's statement when she first heard your name. She said, 'God has provided Jeremy with a helpmate, now he will be all right.' Judy is also a teacher and I can see God's hand in what we strive to do and it gives me new hope."

After Ellen had finished her mission to the mountains and was sure her mind was clear and her spirit renewed, she had another visit to make. Ellen had kept in touch with Amy, the widow of her brother Bruce, and had followed the life of Bruce Wallace, Jr., their only child and her nephew. Bruce was her only blood relative, and she and H.T. had spent hours getting to know him. H.T. had called him a brilliant young man destined for great things. Ellen wanted to talk with Amy first and then with Bruce because he was now a young man. If he was willing, she wanted Con to take him under his wing and teach him the things important about finance. Ellen had a selfish motive here because in the future she hoped Con would slow down and he and Dot could travel with her and Brad. Then one day, when her sons were old enough, Con might want to retire and Bruce could teach his cousins.

Ellen didn't mean to dictate how any of her friends and family lived their lives. Her only desire was to give them the opportunity to make their own decision, something she had not always had. All these people had achieved a lot with what they had to work with, and now she was going to offer them a lot more, so they could achieve even greater things.

Ellen did want one more thing, and that was for Dot to receive the recognition she deserved. Without Dot and her unselfish outlook on life, none of these things she hoped to make possible could ever have come to pass. The school that would be built must be called the Dorothy Clevenger Academy.

Ellen had one other thing she hoped to accomplish. She hoped to persuade Polly to ask Lou to come live with her and help keep the orphanage going. Lou had buried her past and put behind her the violence that had caused her sorrow. Now it was important that she start a new life, and find a place where she was needed. And Polly needed the help if the orphanage was to continue because she was becoming feeble. Ellen only intended to mention these options as suggestions, but felt certain both women would be eager to accept such an arrangement.

Ellen had said she might be gone for six months, but now she hoped to accomplish these things in less than three. She wanted to get back because she was impatient to get on with her life. Brad was waiting, and she needed to start the family she knew could make her life complete. At thirty-five, Ellen had little time to waste if she intended to bear two children—now her first priority.

Yet, Ellen wondered if she were being presumptuous. It could be God might not wish to bless her in this way. Ellen knew this could be a possibility but each time the thought occurred, the memory of her dream returned. Ellen had hoped to feel the presence of Jeremy once she had returned to the mountains, and she had, but she had also felt the presence of Mag. Mag had come to Ellen in a dream and when she told Polly, the old woman responded, "Listen to her message because Mag still lives in two worlds."

In Ellen's dream, Mag spoke to her, saying, "Ellen, God has blessed you and has chosen you to care for one of his special people." Ellen remembered those words because Mag had once spoken them to Polly when Jeremy was left in her care. Ellen tried to tell herself she was simply recalling the story as Polly had told it to her, but each time it came back more clearly in her dream. Ellen wondered if the ways of the mountain people were starting to influence her life, and her way of thinking. She decided it didn't matter. She was sure in her heart God was going to grant her two children, and if one happened to be one of his special people, she would consider that responsibility a privilege.

Ellen was just as certain of something else—if God did choose to bless her with the care of one of his special people, Brad would understand when she named that child Jeremy.

Printed in the United States
131272LV00003BC/4/P